# Jockey School

# JOCKEY SCHOOL

## Michael Feeney Callan

*Based on the television series by Alan Janes*

British Broadcasting Corporation

This story is based on the BBC TV series Jockey School first shown in 1982. It was produced by Paul Stone and directed by Colin Cant. The main characters who appear in the book were played as follows: Billy, Dana Humphries, Tiny, Trevor Wakefield, Phil, Greg Jones, Pete, David Fry, Jack Harrup, Colin Blumenau, Pat Devlin, Desmond Maurer.

Published by the
British Broadcasting Corporation
35 Marylebone High Street
London W1M 4AA

ISBN 0 563 20035 9
© Michael Feeney Callan 1982
© Format and characters Alan Janes 1982
First published 1982

Photoset by
Rowland Phototypesetting Ltd
Bury St Edmunds, Suffolk
Printed in England by
Hollen Street Press
Slough, Berkshire

# ONE

The wind that combed through Tiny's hair and needled through the holes in his jersey was icy cold, but his bones had long ago ceased to rattle. As he crossed the yard and splashed through the black rain puddles he rubbed his eyes, chasing away sleep. It was just gone eleven in the morning, and he was jaded. Already a day's work was behind him. Hours ago, at seven o'clock, when the world was asleep and the moon still shone, he had started the day's labours. As one of the four "lads" at Rectory Training Stables he was in charge of three demanding fillies. That meant that the daily duties of feeding, watering, mucking out, straw-changing and exercising a horse were multiplied threefold. And today was worse. Phil, his mate, was feeling off-colour, so Tiny had agreed to exercise one of his charges as well. Much as he loved horses, and familiar as he was with the routine of mucking out and the rhythm of the ride, Tiny was by now feeling sore and tetchy. He'd ridden out Joy, and Dot and Domino . . . and yet there was more to do. Much more.

He pushed into the big stables, thankful to be free of the wind for a while. In here the warmth of animal flesh radiated, good as any central heating. Tiger Tom, the chestnut gelding, recognised him and gave a short whinny of greeting. Tiny winked, but passed him by. Scribbled in ink on the back of his hand were the names of Phil's important charges, and he consulted these as he moved down the stalls. When he arrived at Eeney's place he was surprised to find Pat Devlin crouched there, hosing down the gelding's foreleg. Pat, a genial Irishman and former jockey, was head stable lad at Rectory. Twice as old as any of the other lads – gone thirty-six – Pat, and his wife Una, had become kind of parent figures to the boys.

Pat looked up with a start as Tiny craned over the door. "What're you doing here? I thought you were supposed to be extra-busy today?"

"I am," Tiny barked back. "Haven't you seen me hefting feed bags since dawn? I've done most of Phil's feeding and now I'm going to ride out some of his horses. Eeney's top of the list. Pete has watered and fed him, so –"

Pat stood and dropped the hose into a bucket. His blue eyes, so strange a match for the gypsy-dark hair, avoided Tiny's. For a second Tiny thought he saw guilt in his expression. "No. You can skip Eeney today. He needs a rest after the Sandown Park race last week."

Although Tiny wasn't normally nosy, he could not help but notice the loop of bandage lying on the ground. He recalled that Phil had not ridden Eeney out yesterday, or the day before. "Is he OK, Pat? I mean – the bandage. I knew there was a mild strain after the race. But I guessed he was fit enough for a walk up and round the back of the village."

Pat fussed. He uncoiled the bandage, shut off the hose, pretended busyness. "He's fine, fine. Just a bit of heat still round the ankle, nothing to worry about. I'll be keeping a close eye on him myself. Phil should have told you that. Don't concern yourself, laddie."

The forced cheerfulness of Pat's tone made Tiny more suspicious, but he obediently turned away. Pat was someone who always called a spade a spade – honest to a fault. If he said the big gelding was fine, then fine of fettle he was! And yet . . . was it Tiny's imagination or had the horse been unstable on that right leg even as they spoke? And yesterday in the course of his work as he blew in and out of the stables, hadn't he noticed how often Eeney had been curled up in the straw instead of standing? And last night in the hostel before lights-out, hadn't Phil said something, expressing concern?

Tiny strolled down the stalls mulling over these issues. If the gelding was unwell then it was bad news indeed for Rectory Stables. Eeney was a prestige horse, a welcome presence in any trainer's stables. Eighteen months ago Vic Favell, Eeney's owner, had graced Rectory with the task of training his horses. He had signed over three, and Jack Harrup, trainer-proprietor of Rectory, had been grateful for the business. From the very first day Eeney had showed best promise. He had inbred talent, and with him came the prospect of reflected glory for Rectory. And though the lads knew little about the boss's finances, it went without saying that the stables could do with a lick of paint and a few pounds spent here and there, and above all with a few winners. So lots of hopes were pinned on Eeney from the beginning. Already he had been raced at top meetings, and his form this season looked excellent. It seemed only a question of time before he won an important race, and Harrup's name as a trainer was made. Everyone had their fingers crossed, nobody more so than the lads, who took pride in their work and, on a more practical level, stood perhaps to gain an extra pound in their thin pay-packets.

The thought of that extra pound was sketching a wry smile on Tiny's face when, out of the blue, a barracks-square voice cut him cold. "What are you up to, mooning about with your hands in your pockets when there's work t'be done, son!"

Tiny glanced round to see Jack Harrup – "Dobbin" to the lads, a barrel-bellied dwarf with a cap of thick hair – strutting towards him. Harrup was fifty-two, with, like so many trainers, an inglorious jockeying career behind him. Tiny had to stop himself exploding. "I'm just about to tack up Tiger Tom and ride him out –"

"Not good enough," Harrup grunted, checking his watch. "Every horse should've been out by eleven. Don't just stand there. Get cracking!"

As Tiny scurried off to the tack room for Tiger Tom's gear, Harrup marched down to Pat. He nudged into Eeney's stall and both men exchanged a tight, uneasy glance. Pat was on his knees again, gently probing the gelding's leg with his fingertips. "Was the boy down here?" Harrup asked brusquely.

"Tiny? Yes, he was. Just helping Phil out. Wanted to exercise Eeney."

Harrup made a throaty sound. "He's too much of a bright spark. Keep him away from here for the moment, till we sort ourselves out." The lined, prematurely-old face was suddenly anxious. "I hope you're looking after Eeney yourself? I don't want the youngsters gossiping among themselves, starting a scare –"

Pat cut in: "In case word gets back to Vic Favell?"

A long, pained sigh escaped Harrup's lips as he stooped to inspect the problem leg. "He's on his way over, Pat. Phoned early on to say he wanted a chat – which probably means he intends to push me to enter Eeney at Worcester next week."

Pat shook his head. "You'll have to tell him, guv'nor. There's a strained tendon here, it could get serious. It'll need time to repair." As he spoke his fingers crossed the centre of pain above the gelding's ankle and the animal shuddered and moaned.

"I know, I know," Harrup mumbled. "But you know what owners are like, Pat. Always impatient! And businessmen like Favell who don't know the first thing about horses are the worst. We'd be flying if it wasn't for that Sandown fiasco. How many times have I told Favell that Eeney can't run on soft ground? Once I saw the rain coming I wanted to pull him off the card."

"But Vic Favell wouldn't have it. And this is the result." Pat's voice was persuasively soft. "So why don't we just come clean? Tell him the going was all wrong at Sandown, but he insisted Eeney run, so he can only blame himself."

"He won't see it like that. Eeney was on form and second favourite. If he sees the injury he'll think the horse's been badly stabled. And he's got two others here, remember. I don't want to give him an excuse to take them away." Harrup began gathering clumps of dry straw and fluffing it up around the injured leg, masking the wet ground. In a rueful voice he added, "I can't afford to lose Vic Favell's business. Believe me."

"The horse isn't ready to race at Worcester," Pat said firmly.

Harrup made a stout-hearted effort to appear unconvinced. He pulled the bandage from Pat's hands and buried it in his overcoat pocket, and made a final adjustment to the little hill of straw built above Eeney's ankle. "At the moment that's only guesswork. We mustn't be too negative. You never know – twenty-four hours and he could be much improved. We haven't had him running yet."

"So you're going to hide the facts from Vic Favell?"

Harrup stood back to examine his handiwork. The gelding was standing squarely and there was no obvious evidence of injury, no bandage mark, no sign of the hose. Pat muffled the little voice of anger that rose within him. It was against his nature to deceive – Vic Favell should know the consequence of the error of his judgement. Eeney should not have run at Sandown, and certainly should not now be running at Worcester. But Pat avoided argument at all costs. After all, the trainer was the boss, he had the last word.

"If circumstances were better I might take a different stance. But right now I just *can't lose* Vic Favell."

"But –" said Pat.

He got no further. They hadn't heard a car, but all of a sudden Vic Favell was striding towards them, chest and head thrust forward like an imperious pigeon. And a fixed look of fury on his face. "Blasted youth!" he snarled. "What are roads for but for driving on!" He addressed a pale-faced Harrup. "The Council should do something about a footpath

9

on that lane that leads down to Rectory. Kids ambling down the middle of the road! What's a man supposed to do – fly over 'em?''

"Bit of bother with one of the lads in the lane, had you?" Harrup couldn't help but stammer.

Favell grimaced. "Not one o' yours, I'm glad to say. Some urchin brat." He shrugged his shoulders as if throwing off the weight of vexation. His eye drifted over Harrup's shoulder and lit upon Eeney. "Ah! There he is, looking strappin' well." Pat and Harrup lurched aside nervously as Favell came into the stall and began circling the gelding, slapping him with affection. "Like I told you last week, I was disappointed by Sandown. He should have finished in the first three. He's going to have to start improving fast."

Harrup was determined to give no ground to Vic Favell: the pretence of confidence must be struck from the start. "Sandown was a top class race. In a lower-grade race Eeney would have finished higher –"

Favell turned away from the horse. Hooking Harrup's arm, he led him out of the stall, towards the privacy of the tack room. His fiery humour had quietened somewhat as he said, "I'm sorry, Jack, but I feel I've given your stables long enough. I've had lots of optimism, but no winning result." Harrup tried to object, but Favell went on: "Now listen. All this has cost me a lot more than I'd anticipated. What with one thing and another, times are hard. For us all, I know. But I'm not in the charity business. I stable my horses here for training and I want winners. It's as simple as that. We failed at Sandown, we failed before. But we can't at Worcester. I'm sorry, but it's got to be a result this time, Jack." When Harrup said nothing Favell added, "Tell me straight: what are Eeney's chances at Worcester?"

There was a hard lump in Harrup's throat but he managed not to choke on it. "G-good. There are some hot things round at the moment, but we don't know if they're going to be running."

"What about a jockey?"

"I'll get the best I can."

Favell was sitting on a stool amid racks of harnesses and saddles. He was silent for a minute, concentrating his attention on the long cheroot he had begun to light. Harrup took in the well-cut tweedy overcoat, the glassy-polished Italian shoes. By contrast his own clothes were cheap and threadbare. And yet Vic Favell was complaining of money troubles! "Unless you tell me differently," Favell said, "I'm going to have to put a wad of notes on Eeney in this race. You see, I need the money to get me out . . . out of a spot of bother." The beady eyes slid back to Harrup's. "But if you tell me *not* to back him, that you think he hasn't an excellent chance of winning, then you've lost all my horses."

"I wouldn't want to do that, Mr Favell."

The cheroot puffed smoke like a train, and Vic Favell eyed his trainer curiously, wondering. One didn't have to be a genius to see that Harrup was tight for cash. The stables seemed well-ordered enough, but there was a clear shortage of equipment and labour. There were twenty horses here, Favell knew, and a staff of only four, not counting Harrup's son, John, an apprentice-jockey himself, but rarely to be seen around. It appeared that Harrup was skint – but then maybe he was just mean! Harrup was a very private man, a hard person to get to know. In his time he had failed as a jockey, yet there were many in the game who said he was a cunning and talented man. Favell had his doubts. On the most basic level, if everything at Rectory was rosy, why wasn't it better staffed?

"Tell me about your lads," Favell said. "You don't keep many?"

Harrup was surprised by this twist in the conversation. Defensively he said, "I have three good lads. I only go for the best. Pete and Phil show real style, they've been promoted to jockey apprenticeships. Tiny's on his month's trial for the same promotion. Pat, of course, is the best possible supervisor. He and Una look after the lads and co-ordinate the whole business. It works very well –"

"But that's not many for all those horses?"

Harrup's face had gone quite red. "No, but we're taking on more. Always on the look-out for bright hard workers, don't y'know. In fact, there's another one starting with us this week . . ."

*

The sight that met Tiny's tired eyes as he trotted Tiger Tom back into the yard shook him back to full alertness. There, in the middle of the bleak flagstones, stood a prim, "civvy" girl. He blinked a few times as he reined in, but she did not disappear. She was small, about sixteen, with a snub-nose and shoulder-length blonde hair. The travel case that stood by her heel was all tidy and proper, just like her pretty face, just like her hair. In fact, he thought to himself, she might have fitted in with the model dummies in the window of a classy High Street fashion shop – if only her coat weren't quite so filthy.

"You lost?" Tiny called out.

The girl's pursed lips hinted at foul humour. She didn't smile. "Not if the sign's right," she returned. "I'm the new stable lass."

"Y-you!" Tiny's jaw hung a mile. Then he chuckled. "Blimey, fancy the guv'nor taking on a girl! There must be a hell of a shortage of lads."

The girl's teeth bared. She wasn't about to be put down by anyone, least of all someone of Tiny's size. "Yes," she rapped, "you're probably right. I suppose that's why he's got a ten-year-old like you riding for him."

"I'm past sixteen," Tiny smarted.

"No kidding?"

Tiny inflated his chest and forced a vicious look, but the girl stood defiant. Chastened, Tiny tugged his mount's bridle, walking him back towards the stable. The girl fell in step, dragging her heavy case. When he saw she wasn't about to be shaken off Tiny reopened the conversation politely. "Have you done much riding?" he said. "These big fellas, I mean. Not ponies."

"I've ridden chasers. I used to work for a farmer every weekend, and he had this point-to-pointer. I was good."

Tiny refrained from challenging her again. They entered the stables and he led Tiger Tom to his stall. The horse stood quietly while Tiny strapped up the stirrups and loosened the girth. The girl had followed him in and stood wide-eyed watching the process. Tiny's eyes roved over her mud-streaked trenchcoat. "How d'you get dirty?" he asked casually.

"Nothin'. Just some stupid car splashed me. It's been raining, you know."

"I know. I was out in it since dawn."

"What you doing?" The girl had ventured close and was following every slick movement of Tiny's hands.

"You're the expert. You ride chasers so well. You should know."

Again the teeth flashed. "I said I'd ridden a chaser. I didn't say I'd done any stabling." There was a breathy pause. "You do understand English?"

By now Tiny was chewing his lip in order to contain his rising anger. "I'm stripping off the saddle, tying up the reins so as he doesn't chew through 'em. Then I'll rub him down, wipe all this sweat off. That'll be it." Tiny set the saddle aside and took up the grooming brush and cloth. The girl had focused all her attention on the horse. With careful, caring hands she stroked the powerful animal's neck and shoulder. Her soothing whispers were a far cry from the sarcastic way she spoke to Tiny. "You'd better get on to talk to Dobbin, the boss," Tiny said. "I think that's his voice I can hear from the far end of the stable, from the tack room."

"In a minute. Could I . . ." She was observing Tiny rub the gelding down. "Could I try that? Just a little bit?"

"Why?"

For a moment there had been gentleness and enthusiasm in the girl's voice. But as soon as she saw Tiny's cynical grin, and guessed he was taking advantage of her softening tone, she became fierce again. "All right, keep your job to yourself. Put your back into it. Drop dead for all I care!"

"Keep your shirt on!" Tiny backed off. "I was only askin'." He held out the folded pad of cloth. "You've never tended a horse proper before, eh? Here, have a go. Nice and easy now."

The girl took the cloth and began gingerly rubbing the horse down. A sight she looked, Tiny thought to himself – with her wind-blown hair and belted coat and trim slacks. And that earnest look of happy concentration pasted all over her face. But her touch was good, he saw. Tiger Tom, normally as frisky as a day-old kitten, stood still. Few people possessed the gift of controlling this big 'un, but she had the touch all right. "What's your name anyhow?" Tiny asked.

"Hilary – but everyone calls me Billy."

"That's an odd name for . . ." Tiny stopped himself just in time. He folded his arms and began humming gently to himself. Talking to this girl was like trying to converse with a rumbling volcano. After a few minutes the horse was dried and groomed and beginning to get restless. "That'll do for the moment. He'll be a bit chilly so I'll throw the rug over him now and then he'll be ready for a small feed." Billy helped spread the warm rug. She was clearly enjoying herself, and taking the learning seriously. Working shoulder to shoulder with her wasn't so bad, Tiny reflected. Maybe she would fit in after all. She seemed screwy enough to be welcome at Rectory – Tiny had a long-held belief that you had to be a bit crazy to exist here. Why else would the lads put up with a twelve-hour day, a grubby live-in hostel and a miserable weekly reward? Watching Billy's cheery-faced excitement, he suddenly felt sorry for her. It wouldn't be easy, trying to make a go of it at Rectory. It was tough enough for hardy boys. What would it be like for a girl? And what would *she* be like after a few mornings of six-thirty alarm calls and cockroaches under the bed? It was no fun mucking out a filthy stable at dawn with your breakfast toast still clamped in your teeth. But if she really was mad and brave enough . . . well, who knows, she might even hold on for a season. They could take bets on it up at the hostel. Pat wouldn't play, but Phil and Pete could be in on it. Tiny imagined the stakes: *a pound says she lasts a month*. That'd be Phil. But Tiny would top that: *three quid says she makes it till Easter*!

Tiny pulled himself out of his rambling reverie. "Would you like to get the corn for him?" he asked Billy. "It's across in the feed room. And while you're going over, close the main stables door, will you? It's nippy today and we don't want any draughts causing colds for these fellas."

Billy ran off, delighted to be involved, but was back in seconds – minus the corn bag. Tiny immediately recognised panic on her face. "What's the matter?" he mumbled.

She could barely string the words together. "That car outside, parked behind the Landrover. I didn't see it when we came in. The red Rover saloon. W-who owns it?"

Tiny raised his shoulders. "Dunno, didn't notice it. It's probably some feed rep. We get plenty of them, 'cause there's so many stables around here." He thought twice. "Then again – a red Rover, you say? That might be a business friend of the guv'nor's –"

They were standing at the entrance to Tiger Tom's stall, looking down the length of the stable towards the tack room and rear office. Suddenly two figures emerged from the tack room and Billy's heart sank. "Oh no!" she exclaimed, clutching her mouth. In a fast sweep she grabbed Tiny's arm and dragged him bodily into the stall. "Quick," she hissed, "you've got to cover me. That man – he'd better not see me."

Confused, Tiny merely stuttered, "What man? Dobbin? He's the guv'nor. You've got to face *him* –"

Billy dropped on her hunkers and pulled Tiny's small

body in front of her like a shield. They edged into the far corner of the stall, behind the horse. "No, not him. Now just shut up. Don't attract attention. Let them pass and maybe they won't look in."

"But what's wrong? If it's not Dobbin, why d'you want to hide from Mr Favell? He owns some of the horses here—"

"Oh dear . . . keep still, will you, and *hush!*" Billy's voice was electric.

Vic Favell and Harrup were wrapped in conversation and would probably have walked past but for Tiger Tom's interruption. Seeing another familiar face the gelding geared forward, neighing excitedly. Harrup was pleased about the distraction. Favell had been back on his hobbyhorse, querying and beefing about what he contended were mis-judgements in the training schedules. But when he saw his other gelding he was diverted. He moved to greet Tiger Tom, patting his head. "Here's another one that could perk up a bit," he griped. "He's shown no form at all yet. I don't know what you've been doing with 'im."

"As a matter of fact, I've great plans for Tiger Tom. I'm planning giving him an outing at . . ." Harrup stopped dead. As the horse's rump shifted he could see a red-faced and very awkward-looking Tiny propping the partition at the back of the stall. "What are you doin' there, son?"

"Er, nothing. I . . . I just finished rubbing him down."

Tiger Tom sidled left again and Harrup and Favell had a better view. Tiny wasn't the only body poised in the shadows. There was another leg stirring, and an oddly protruding elbow. "What the hell are you playing at, lad? Who's there behind you? I can see a fawn-coloured coat quite clearly. Stand away."

Billy was clinging tight to the tail of Tiny's jersey. Tiny whispered, "Sorry," and stepped aside. Billy cringed, but drew herself up, preparing for the storm.

"*You!*" Vic Favell gasped. He shook his birdlike head in

disbelief and swung on Harrup. "Does this . . . *person* work here?"

Harrup eyed Billy, remembering their interview in London, her excellent references. Yes, she was much as he remembered her, though when they'd last met she was considerably cleaner-looking. He noted that she was a few hours early. "You're Hilary Ure," he said. She nodded in shamed silence. "She's to be my new stable help," he told Favell. He turned back to the girl. "But what are you doing out here? Why didn't you go up to the house, like I instructed?"

Billy had no chance to answer. Vic Favell's expression grew darkly severe and he prodded a stubby finger towards her. "Harrup, if this is the kind of person you have, or plan to have looking after my horses – well, it's no wonder things are slack around here."

Harrup was annoyed. "Nothing's slack around here, Mr Favell."

"Winners are slack enough, I'd say." The veins were standing out on Favell's forehead. "This, let me tell you, is an ill-mannered, badly-bred scamp! Do you know what she called me, not a half-hour ago? In this very lane outside, not a mile up, she had the audacity to call me a stupid pig and a fat idiot. Screamed it, she did! Well, sir, I may be both, especially for keeping my horses here. But I don't need a rascal like her to announce it to the world."

Harrup's head was spinning. The half-hour of intrigue over Eeney was about enough, thank you, for one morning. He could do without this flare-up. He fixed on Billy. "Did you say these things?"

Billy blurted out, "It's not fair! He's not telling the full story. The roads were full of rain puddles and I'd been walking since I got off the Sparsholt bus. You know what the lane is like – all potholes. I was keeping in to the edge, then he thunders past like he owns the place. He didn't look out. He splashed dirty water all over my new coat. Just look! I

17

shouted after him and he stopped and got out and shouted back at me. He was rude –''

Vic Favell would hear no more. "The bare-faced cheek," he said. He tugged Harrup's sleeve. "I've never been so insulted. If this girl works here, Jack, I see no future relationship between us. Not from this day on. As far as I'm concerned she'll just be a symbol of everything that's wrong with the stables."

"Right, I take your point. She's obviously not got the temperament needed for looking after horses –''

In that split-second Billy saw her proposed job, with all her hopes and ambitions tagged on, fizzle like a spent rocket. Rage welled inside her and she called out wildly: "There's another reason I said those things: he *is* a stupid pig!''

Tiny stifled a nervy giggle but Harrup was appalled. "You're sacked," he snapped.

"I haven't started yet," Billy retorted. "So how can I be sacked?''

"Don't dare cheek me, girl. Go outside and wait for me. I'll give you your fare home."

Billy appeared to fight back the words that were tumbling to her lips. Very pale, she pulled herself proudly upright, and walked from the stall. She wouldn't have revealed it to anyone – nor admitted it to herself even – but there was a tear at the corner of her eye. It was all so unfair, she told herself. Maybe she had flown into a fury, but this Mr Favell had been careless and quite rude in the lane. Had she no right to speak up for herself? Why shouldn't she say what she truly felt? But the really sad part was that she had built her hopes up for this job, day-dreaming for the four months since she'd left school, saving her pocket money, conniving with her young brothers to persuade Dad to allow her to make the long journey from Burnham to Sparsholt village on the edge of the Lambourn downs to embark on a career she really wanted. If Mum were alive it might have been easier. For three years she had been a substitute Mum to the family; but at last the boys were old enough to look after themselves. And so her chance had come. Incredibly, the first job she applied for, the one she really fancied, had been offered to her. Rectory Stables – a racing stables – the ideal first base for the plans she had in mind. Honest determination had helped her find her way here, and now an honest burst of temper was flinging her out. It was enough to make the toughest girl break down and cry.

Billy stood outside the big stable door with her case and listened to Harrup inside, gushing out apology. So they had nicknamed him "Dobbin". Dobbin meant "workhorse". The old nag. How fitting, Billy thought cruelly – because from out here he sounded like a limp-spirited old dullard – *Yes, Mr Favell, no, Mr Favell, three bags full, Mr Favell.* "I'm terribly sorry for all this," he was blethering. "I'm only glad I found out exactly what she was like before we signed papers . . ."

After a minute the two men came out into the yard. Harrup made an attempt to shake Vic Favell's hand, but his gesture was ignored. Favell said, "Keep me closely informed about Worcester. I'll expect a phone call, all the details."

"Of course. Rely on me."

Favell grunted and climbed into his car. As the door banged shut Billy felt Harrup nudge her softly on the arm. She looked up, but his eyes were trained away from hers. Did he even notice she was there? But all of a sudden he was saying, very quietly lest anyone else overhear: "What did you call him? The truth – come on, out with it."

"A stupid great pig," Billy's voice trembled.

"What else?"

"A fat idiot."

Favell's car drew level with them, rolling slowly towards the gate. Harrup gave a wide smile and a friendly wave. As he did, through clenched teeth, he murmured to Billy, "Well, my girl, you're absolutely right on both counts. You've described him to a tee."

Astonished, Billy stumbled back against the stable door.

Before Favell's Rover had turned the corner he said, "Go and find the head man. His name is Pat Devlin. He and his wife live in the bungalow over there. You'll be in the hostel behind. Pat'll show you the score round here."

"But you sacked me."

"Well, I've rehired you, haven't I? Just make sure you keep out of the way when that fool comes round again." Billy nodded enthusiastically. But Harrup's smile had faded. "And do something about that big mouth of yours, will you!"

# TWO

"Who's the girl?" Phil asked, tugging the heavy blanket tight about him as though to ward off further assault from the germs threatening him.

"What girl?" Pete, the solemn, quiet one, allowed his curiosity to get the better of him. He moved over to join Phil by the window of the hostel's living-room. It was lunchtime and the gas stove had been burning for hours, but still it was cold. In winter the hostel was always cold, so run-down was it. Even in the mildest breeze floorboards creaked, doors rattled and windows whistled. Today the tangle of noises was wild and endless, like the sound of an old ship under full sail. Phil held the blanket under his chin and nodded towards the object of his interest. By the corner of the Devlins' bungalow they could just see her, chatting with Una, Pat's wife. The girl was pulling on riding boots and beside her, tied to the railing of the big stable, stood Gobbledegook, the ill-trained young gelding everyone loved to hate. "I reckon she's an owner's daughter or something," Pete said, and he slumped down in a chair to return to his cheese sandwich.

"But it looks like she's going to ride Gobbledegook, with Pat or Una's blessing. Gobbledegook's owner would know better. To give you credit, Pete, you're the only one who can really hold that horse."

Pete grunted, but did not argue the truth. Just then Tiny arrived, wind-blown and blue in the face. The tea flasks and sandwiches Una had prepared decorated the huge central table, kept company by a variety of ashtrays, racing papers, toffee wrappings and other junk. Tiny rummaged for food. He had heard Phil's remarks about Gobbledegook and the new girl and noted the look of bemused wonder on his face. He explained, "That's our extra help, the new 'lad'. Her name's Billy, believe it or not."

"Strewth!" Phil gasped. "A female lad! And Pat's trying her on Gobbledegook."

"A good match, I'd say," Tiny chuckled grimly as he poured his tea. "Two deadly little brats. You should have seen what I saw this morning. She arrived, insulted an owner, got promptly sacked. Then, bingo. She's promptly rehired!"

Phil shook his head in a world-weary way. "The ways of women. Sweet-talked old Dobbin, I suppose." He sounded dismayed. "But a *girl* on the team – well, it's just too much. Dobbin must have really lost his marbles –"

"Or else she's very good," Pete put in softly.

Pete's sudden contributions to conversation never failed to surprise. He was the stables' star apprentice and showed all the signs of becoming a fine jockey one day. But he was moody and serious-minded, and often made glum company. Harrup – and even Phil, for that matter – were often impatient with him to the point of unfriendliness. But Tiny believed in the "live and let live" principle and respected him for what he was – a brilliant but shy young man who, all told, preferred the company of horses to that of people. Tiny also admired Pete's keen sense of understanding people's motives and methods. Harrup, he knew, would not have engaged Billy unless her references were first-class. But what was his plan for her? Hardly that she should ever be more than a stable lass, Tiny assumed. Most lads came to racing stables as a first step on the ladder to becoming jockeys – but surely not her. Of course there were girl jockeys, but they were few and far between. And none ever came from Rectory Stables. Tiny pushed the girl out of his mind and concentrated on the other event of the morning, the suspicions about Eeney's health. He gave a straight account of his fears to Pete and Phil and concluded, "After the chat with Pat I had my doubts about the gelding's leg, but then I overheard Dobbin tell Pat that Eeney would positively be entered for Worcester next week. Pat wasn't happy about it at all. When I came on the scene he shut up, but I could quite easily tell."

"I fed him this morning," Pete said. "But he's not my horse."

All eyes moved to Phil. Phil nervously tugged at his hair, a gesture of habit and concern. "I've been troubling over Eeney myself all week, but Pat's been keeping me otherwise occupied. It seemed every time I went anywhere near him Pat was on the spot telling me to fetch or do something else. I saw the bandage go on, of course. But Pat said it was only a small strain. I rode him out once, on Monday, but the rain washed us out. He was slow, but it was hard to tell anything for certain. Eeney hates the rain. So Pat wouldn't let him out yesterday."

Pete finished his cheese sandwich and burrowed into a movie magazine. To no one in particular he said, "Well, the guv'nor won't take risks with valuable horses like Eeney. If he's declaring him for Worcester the gelding *must* be all right."

"And Pat wouldn't lie to us," Phil added, a shade uncertainly. He crumpled in a stove-side chair and toasted his hands. "That's why *I* put it to the back of my mind. Pat wants to take charge of Eeney for a while – fine. There's no more experienced, more decent chap for the job." He grinned. "Present company excluded." Phil saw that Tiny was still bothered. "Anyhow, a strain's not the end of the world. It'll mend. Worcester is a bit away yet."

Tiny shrugged and sipped tea. "I know. But it worries me because we all know Rectory needs a winner. Eeney's the one that's been moving towards victory. There's nothing else in the stables that comes anywhere near him."

Pete and Phil fell silent, both staring at Tiny, remembering their own share of responsibility in failure or success. For a few minutes there was a heavy, depressed silence. "I wonder who the guv'nor'll choose to ride Eeney at Worcester?" Pete said. "Phil and I are due a ride, so it will probably be either of us."

Phil looked anxious. Then he plucked up and made an effort to dispel the gloomy atmosphere Tiny had brought with him. "Worcester's next week's worry. What about today? What about this Gilly or Billy, or whatever her name is?" He clapped his hands with gaiety. "She'll probably be taking Gobbledegook round the manege, maybe trying the hurdles. Why not let's go down and have a peek? Get a laugh out of it, I'll bet!"

No one stirred. Pete went back to the new movie reviews. "I'll stay here, thanks. Enjoy my lunch break. Lord knows we don't get much time to ourselves."

Tiny made himself comfortable, poured more tea and lit a cigarette. He wouldn't be moved either. Phil gave a despondent sigh and resigned himself. "Umm. Probably right," he decided. "Who wants to see some stupid girl fall on her backside?" Restless, he crossed back to the window and rubbed away the condensation. The girl had vanished from sight, but he could hear the clopping of hooves as Gobbledegook crossed the yard.

In the manege, just as the lads supposed, Pat Devlin was getting ready to put Billy through her paces. As he watched her mount up, he was a little sceptical about the whole business. He had known the boss was looking for new help at the stables and had been consulted about one or two applications, but nothing had prepared him for a girl. He recalled the applications he had seen. None indicated experience of horses. Perhaps this was the reason the girl got the job – apparently she had worked with horses before. Pat smiled to himself. And probably, he thought, she works cheap.

Billy was having a hard time keeping Gobbledegook calm.

The black horse was constantly bucking. But she kept a short rein and fastened her legs close to his sides.

"All right," Pat began, "you say you can ride well. The purpose of this little try-out is to show me your capabilities. Being a stable lass involves more than just exercising the horses, of course. But the ability to ride well is vital. I want to see Gobbledegook work *with* you, I want to see him respond to your guidance, trust you. OK?"

Billy's confidence – wounded in the row with Favell – was bubbling again. She felt at home in the saddle and the muscular power of the animal under her was not in the least bit frightening. Gobbledegook lurched to dart away, but she tugged him back sharply. "I know what I'm doing," she said smartly. Then she flicked the reins and prodded the horse's sides. As if suddenly wary of the girl's strength of will, Gobbledegook moved off carefully, walking at a smooth brisk pace. The angry bumping had ceased completely.

Pat jumped up on the fence that surrounded the training ring and folded his arms in concentration. "Just walk him round for a bit, let him get to know you. Talk to him, tell him how handsome he is. That'll keep him in the right mood."

"Yes, yes. I know."

The tart smugness of Billy's voice irritated Pat, but he simply shook his head. He had seen many lads pass through this same ritual at Rectory over the years. He had listened to the cleverboots big-mouths . . . and picked them up from the dirt where, almost invariably, they landed themselves. Was Billy to be another?

"All right," he shouted. "Start rising now."

Billy goaded Gobbledegook into a trot, as commanded. The horse was edgy and the saddle rather too square, but Billy found her rhythm quickly and the trot was good. "Fine," Pat was calling out. "Keep him round the edge, away from the jumps in the middle. I don't want you to jump." Billy scarcely heard a word. The wintry breeze was in her ears and, anyway, a mood of jubilant excitement had overtaken her. For all she knew just then she might have been a thousand miles from Rectory. "Come on, boy," she urged Gobbledegook. "Keep smooth. Head up, even gait." And the horse obeyed her. This is living, she thought. This is what I came here for. This is worth all the haggling with Dad, the long journey, the saving up, the dreaming. For a second her mind dashed back to the quarrel with Favell and the boss. To think how close she came to losing everything! All because of her stupid temper. Silently she cursed herself and, without thinking, spurred the horse harder. Gobbledegook's gait stretched to a canter, moving fast.

Pat was about to shout, to check Billy, but Jack Harrup drew up by the manege fence. The old man glanced towards the girl. "She seems OK," he remarked. "Sturdy looking kid. She'll fit in once that chip's knocked off her shoulder."

"Her application was good?"

"The best. Excellent school reports. She had three varied part-time jobs, all around farms. Seems to enjoy hard work." He nodded forward. "And there's no doubt she can hold a saddle." Pat wanted to ask more questions but Harrup changed the subject. "Listen," he said. "I want you to prepare a training programme for Eeney for Worcester. Whether anyone likes it or not, the horse will be running."

"But guv'nor, he's not fit. Taking him up to the gallops tomorrow would be very risky."

"So?" Harrup shrugged. "Risk is the name of the game. Odds, gambles, risks. As an ex-jockey you should know that, Pat." He held up a hand to stop any argument. "I've made my case to you. *I* agree it's not too wise. But Vic Favell has left us with no choice. I won't go into the finer details, but it's enough to say that Favell *has to* run the horse. And I can't afford to pull against him. So that's the end of it, Pat. Eeney will have to be taken out. He'll have to face the gallops tomorrow, and a tight training schedule after that."

Harrup was gone before Pat could object further. Pat was annoyed and his attention drifted, but then he noticed that

Billy was romping round the ring, moving very fast, apparently lost in her own world. She had ceased following the correct course and was criss-crossing. Pat stood high on the fence and yelled, "Ease him back, Billy. He's had enough for the moment." He watched and waited. Billy ignored him. She took Gobbledegook into a wide cantering arc, following the fence for twenty yards then rushing towards the centre of the manege. Pat understood at the last second what she was about to do. The hurdles were up and she was making for them. "No!" he hollered. "I don't want you to jump him!"

But Billy was already braced for the jump. Gobbledegook came in with measured exactness, leapt up and cleared the first hurdle perfectly. The second was trickier. It was close, higher and at an awkward angle. But Billy wanted that one too. Without a flicker of nervousness she pulled Gobbledegook round and raced him over the third jump. This time the landing was hard and the horse's pace slackened automatically as he came down. Pat was across the manege in a flash, grabbing Gobbledegook's reins and pulling him up. "What're you playing at?" he demanded. "I told you not to jump."

Billy seemed to shake herself awake. "Oh, er . . . I didn't hear you. Sorry."

"You heard me all right. You just didn't bother to listen."

"I said I'm sorry." Billy's tone was bitter.

"I think you were trying to impress me and the guv'nor. Is that it?"

"The fences were there, so I jumped them. I don't see what all the alarm bells are for."

"Get down."

He held the horse while she slid off expertly, avoiding the amateur's trap of using the stirrup. She turned to face him with a sheepish gaze. Pat took the horse away from her. "I don't often lose my temper, Billy. You just ask one of the lads when I last raised my voice at 'em. But the lads are serious workers. They know they must do what they're told – and they do. Some people are good on horses without knowing much about them. You haven't worked at a stables, and this is your first day here. You have a lot to learn. You can hurt yourself badly in this game. Come off a mount badly and you can break your neck, break your back, and find you're spending the rest of your life in a wheelchair. I *know* people who've suffered like that. Then you can try something fancy and damage the horse. Damage him seriously and he has to be shot. Even the simplest of injuries can ruin his racing career. That means an investment of thousands of pounds down the drain for some owner, and unnecessary agony for some poor beast . . ." Pat could see he was hitting home. Billy's head hung and she looked shocked. But Pat pressed on: "You may think you're special. But then everyone does in their own way. That doesn't exclude you from having to obey rules. You *must* do what you are told."

Of course the basis of what Pat was saying was true, Billy knew. She had been trying to show off, and she had been reckless. It was silly to try to jump a horse you didn't know. Rectory Stables was proving quite a testing ground for her. Here was another crisis, the second in three hours! She could hear Pat breathing hard, but she was afraid to look up.

After a minute he said, "I think I understand. You're not here to be a stable 'help' at all, are you? It's a jockey apprenticeship you're after? You've set your sights on the racing game."

Billy met his gaze boldly at last and the answer was in her eyes. Pat let out a long sigh. Female jockey, he thought to himself – what a target for any girl to set herself! True, there were harder jobs to capture: like female astronaut, for example. He smiled and, just for an instant, felt something close to admiration for this angry little imp. "Aye," he said. "You have some talent. Maybe you'll make it, maybe not. But you have a long way to go. Take my advice. Step by step learn to jump the fences, not *build* them."

"Hmm."

"I'll assume that's a 'yes, Pat'. Now. Una tells me you haven't yet formally met the other lads. So let me bring you across to your new home and introduce you."

Billy was suddenly very polite. "Where will I be sleeping?" she asked.

"In the hostel, you'll have a room to yourself. For the rest you'll muck in with the boys. Una prepares dinner each evening, so you join us then in the bungalow." Pat tousled her hair, begging a smile. "You may even enjoy yourself here."

"Hmm. I'll enjoy Tiger Tom and Gobbledegook and . . ." She reached out to take the horse's reins. "May I?" Pat handed over the leathers and they turned to walk back towards the yard and stables, their shadows lengthening on a winter's afternoon that had already become evening.

*

That evening and the next day were times of excitement and disruption at Rectory, not only for Billy but for everyone else as well. For Billy the business of meeting people, finding her feet and settling in was exhausting. She was a girl in a man's world, and every step of the way seemed a struggle. Una stayed in the background and didn't interfere. But Billy was ready and able for challenges. Having broken the ice with Pat she wasted no time in letting Harrup know of her ambitions. His response was discouraging, if not negative. Mr Harrup, it seemed, had other things on his mind and no time to chat with her. Those other things involved the re-organisation of the stable duties, which affected everybody. Responsibility for looking after the horses was to be reshuffled between Pete, Tiny, Phil, Billy and John, Harrup's son. Most of the lads got different charges but, for the moment, no one was given Eeney. So the following day was a frantic jumble of mixed work with little time for talk. It was just as well that everyone was kept busy because at every opportunity, Billy sensed, the

29

boys were ready to tackle and tease her.

The second night in the hostel, unlike the first, Billy slept well. At the unearthly hour of six-thirty the alarm went off and she fell groggily out of bed. Dazed, she pulled on jeans and jumper, washed and shambled out to the living-room. Three dead-eyed faces turned towards her. Pete was boiling up a few eggs on the ancient stove. Phil was muffling himself up to face his first day's serious work since Saturday. Tiny was half-interestedly watching *Biology: Form and Function*, the Open University programme on early morning television. Everyone looked as bad as Billy felt. Her head ached and her back was stiff from endless mucking yesterday. She couldn't help but groan aloud.

"Too much for you already, eh?" Phil made an effort to grin but gave up half-way. He could barely keep his own eyes open.

Billy flopped down by the table, straining to appear alert and content. She knew they still viewed her with suspicion but was determined to overcome this. Phil and Tiny were staring at her but she diverted them by asking, "Does John Harrup have to follow the same timetables as us?"

"Ha!" Tiny caught the scalding hard-boiled egg Pete threw to him. "John Harrup work! Now there's a novel thought." Gripping the egg with the edge of his jersey he started to work on it with a spoon. "John has all the privileges of being the boss's son. A big comfy bed in the manor house across the yard, all that. Plus he's got a kinda' ring through Dobbin's nose, far as we can see. He's a shrewd dog, is old John. He wants to be a jockey, so Dad gives him the leg-up, makes him an apprentice just like that." Tiny snapped his fingers. "But the truth of it is he has no talent. Anyone'd out-ride him. Even . . ." Tiny was looking for the most outlandish example . . . "even you."

Phil joined Tiny's loud laughter but Billy was not amused. "You might be very surprised how well I can ride." She chewed her lip. "But it all depends on when I get the chance to try, doesn't it? Yesterday I never left the stables. You all had rides, but I was kept indoors mostly."

Tiny and Phil swung on her, looking scornful and shocked. "Easy does it, Miss Greedy," Phil snapped. "A stable help is a stable help. He, or she, starts with the feeding and mucking. You may have had farm experience, but you've lots to learn about stabling horses. If and when Pat Devlin thinks you're right – when you've learned enough – he'll probably let you start exercising horses. But that may be a long, long time. I reckon best you'll do for a month or two is walk horses round the yard –"

"Never!" Billy spat the word and almost missed catching the boiled egg Pete flicked to her. "I'm no five-year-old. I came to learn all right, but I expect to see my talent used properly."

The harshness of Billy's voice warned Phil and Tiny off. They dug into their eggs and bread without another word. Pete stayed on his feet. He ate his egg in a hurry and brewed some tea. When he was finished, without speaking, he pulled on his anorak and left. Billy watched him go. Of the boys he was the least insulting, and the best rider. Yesterday she had watched him ride out. His unshowy expertise impressed her, but when she tried to compliment him he reacted quite rudely, stomping away as though her comments meant nothing. Now Billy said, "He's an odd one, isn't he? Is he always so wrapped up in himself?"

"Who? Pete?" Tiny shrugged. "Reckon he has the best attitude. He prefers talking to horses than to people. He thinks they make more sense."

Billy ignored the obvious jibe. When she finished eating she pulled her chair near the stove to warm herself but Phil advised her: "I wouldn't take root there if I were you. It's gone seven. If Pat Devlin finds you you'll be out on your ear." He began wriggling into his padded leather jacket. Then, with a final adjustment to his woollen cap, he plunged out into the cold. Tiny switched off the television and made a token effort at cleaning up the cups and spoons while Billy brooded. Almost as if he was purposely rubbing salt into wounds he said, "This'll be your job from now on. The breakfast-making. Phil and Pete do it once a week each, while I do the other five days. But now I'll do once a week as well, and you'll do the rest."

"You're joking."

"I'm not, you know. Remember you're the newcomer. Phil and Pete have been here several months. They are advanced apprentice jockeys. I'm on my month's trial, then I'll be an apprentice too. Which leaves you as the kid. Right?"

Billy held back. Breakfast-making and muck-raking! She might as well be back home, looking after the family and working at weekends for Farmer Doran. Tiny was standing there, bracing himself for an outburst, but none came. Like the volcano, she merely grumbled. Would she last the course till Easter, he asked himself.

"Better not sit around much longer," Tiny cautioned as he made for the door. "The one thing no one will tolerate in racing stables is late starters. And you're late already. On your second day."

A starlit sky greeted Tiny as he walked outside. There was no rain, just that ever-present, bitter wind. In the east the grey light of dawn was seeping from the hills. Tiny's body registered the cold with a shudder then, in a trick of self-control mastered weeks ago, abruptly switched off. From now on he would function like a well-oiled robot, feeling nothing, merely performing duties. With luck, before his senses crept back to life with the hunger pangs of mid-morning, all the heavy work would be completed.

He was just about to enter the enclosed stable when Pat Devlin approached. Pat looked up to the stars, as though estimating the time. "Where's Billy? She understands her work load, I presume? Tending the fillies in the lower stalls?"

"She's on her way," Tiny said loyally.

"Everything OK?" Pat prodded. He trusted Tiny.

Tiny nodded. "I guess she's just a bit unsettled because . . . well, I get the impression she's not used to being the junior. *She* wants to be making the decisions and striking the pace."

"I dare say you're right. I gather her home life hasn't been the easiest. Her Mum died and since then she's had to care for a young family. Tough on her. And bear in mind what this business must seem like to a newcomer – and a girl. The army'd be a hundred times easier!"

So Pat was defending her already. Well, in spite of everything – and though she might not know it – she was making progress.

They walked down the big stable and Tiny went to turn towards his first stall but Pat held his arm. "I want to chat with you about Eeney," Pat explained. "Let's look him over." They went into the gelding's enclosure and bent down beside Eeney's bandaged leg. Tiny knew he was in for some honest truths, and his heart was beating fast. Pat stripped off the bandage and examined the leg. He clicked his tongue. "Feel that, just above the fetlock. There's a wide sensitive area with a fair bit of heat still." His eyes moved slowly up to meet Tiny's. "You may as well know the facts. None of you are fools and I'm sure you've been guessing at it: Eeney seems to have suffered a deep tendon strain at Sandown. There's some improvement, but . . . well, the guv'nor's declaring him at Worcester next week, so I have to start up a training programme. I tried to give him a run yesterday but it was impossible with that misty rain. I didn't push it and I couldn't judge anything. Today's much better. So I want you to take him up to the gallops. I'll drive up to watch you, and Mr Harrup probably will too."

Tiny's eyes searched deep. "You're worried, I can tell. But you made a bit of a secret about all this."

"That wasn't me, Tiny. It was the guv'nor. And it's understandable. He's been under pressure from Vic Favell and he was afraid of ugly rumours starting. You know how word travels in the village pubs. I don't mistrust any of you, but slips can be made. And Eeney is an important horse." He saw that Tiny still wasn't satisfied. Finally he admitted, "I am quite worried. This is the sort of borderline injury you just never know with. Hard exercise might heal it overnight. I've seen it happen. I've also seen irreparable damage caused by racing a horse in this condition."

Tiny slapped the gelding affectionately. "And Worcester is unavoidable?"

"Yes." Pat stood and dusted off his hands. His manner discouraged further questions. "Now, where's the rest of the lads? May as well fix a team to ride out to the gallops. I want to have a look at Phil's form too –"

"Mightn't that be unwise, Pat? I mean, there's bound to be schools from other stables up there too. If everyone sees Eeney – ?"

"In for a penny, in for a pound. It can't make any difference at this late stage. If he runs lame, well, that's scotched any hopes of Worcester."

"Where does that leave the guv'nor with Vic Favell?"

"I don't know, Tiny. That's not really any of our business. Let's keep our minds on our own duties, eh?"

Leaving Tiny to clean out Eeney's stall, Pat strolled off in search of the others. Pete and Phil's voices could be heard coming from the feed room, but before he reached it he came upon Billy, looking for some muck sacks. Not ten minutes out, she was already filthy. Unhappiness was painted all over her face. She veered towards him.

" 'Scuse me, Pat – but when's Mr Harrup going to have that talk with me? I don't mean to sound impatient but it's false pretences if I stay on without making it perfectly clear that I want an apprenticeship."

"Mr Harrup has a lot on his mind right now."

"Maybe. But I . . ." She looked hurt. "The boys treat me like some dumb parlour maid. I want *them* to know – "

Pat smiled. That disarming, sheepish gaze she wore had a

way of softening him in seconds. "Very well. Leave it with me. I'll talk to him today."

"Thanks."

He moved to go, but paused. "What're you up to now?"

"Muckin'."

"Like to ride your friend out?"

"What? Gobbledegook?"

Pat nodded. "Phil will muck him out. You finish the fillies, then tack him up and join us in the yard in half an hour. We're going up to the gallops . . ."

Billy ceased listening. The *gallops*. The trainer's testing ground! Her heart skipped. She had a lot to do in half an hour, but suddenly there were wings on her heels.

# THREE

Harrup's Landrover bumped up to the gravel pitch at the edge of the gallops. He stepped down with his son John and joined an apprehensive-looking Pat Devlin. Pat lowered his binoculars and gestured forward. The vast treeless tract that was the gallops spread before them like an emerald desert. In the far distance could be seen the ant-like figures of riders from neighbouring stables. Away to the left, along one of the marked runs, a solitary horseman was visible.

"That's Tiny," Pat explained. "Coming towards us now. I sent the other team – Phil, Pete and the girl – across the far side for the moment. I thought you wouldn't want to be distracted."

"How's he doing? You haven't tried to jump him I hope?" The words came out in short airy bursts. Harrup pulled his soft hat down over his eyes and bit a fingernail nervously. Beside him fair-haired John was, as always, the picture of relaxation. He leant casually on the bonnet of the Landrover.

"He's not attempting anything fancy. Just a gallop. As it was, I had reservations about allowing that. The ground's still soft – softer than I thought."

"Not a lot we can do about that, Pat. We have to start exercising him sometime or he'll have no breath for the race." Harrup borrowed Pat's binoculars and trained them on the approaching rider. "Looks smooth," he mumbled. "But the boy's only cantering."

Tiny rode up and reined in before the group. He glanced

apologetically round. "He was even on his step, guv'nor, but I certainly didn't have to hold 'im back. He didn't seem much bothered about running, even with the whip."

"Blast!" Pat crouched to check over the strained leg. At least, Pat thanked his lucky stars, a rough examination showed no deterioration. The gelding appeared to be in no pain.

"Give him a chance to warm up," Harrup said. "Trot him a bit, keep his head up and don't let him dictate pace. Keep him busy for ten minutes – "

"You want me to have a try?" John interrupted, not greatly bothered either way, his attention latched on the banana he was peeling.

"Why?" his father barked. "You suppose you can work miracles?"

Pat was well aware of the delicate love-hate relationship between Harrup and his lazy son. Before the storm had a chance to brew he cut in: "Tiny's the ideal weight for this situation. He knows Eeney a little better too – with due respect, John. I think it's best to let him ride this session."

John snorted and turned indifferently away. Satisfied, Tiny kicked Eeney and they moved off at a slow pace. Harrup toyed with the binoculars, holding back temper and nerves. "Which other horses are out?" he asked.

"Domino, Lady Laughter and Gobbledegook. The girl's on Gobbledegook."

"Brave girl." Harrup almost conceded a chuckle. "Where exactly are they? Can you point 'em out?"

Pat scanned the horizon for the black gelding and Billy's yellow jersey. "I think that might be our lads over there. Looks like they're with a group from another stables."

Just as Harrup was focusing the glasses, a spiralling argument was beginning on the far circuit. The Rectory group had mixed in with a team from the nearby Shentons' Stables and Billy had promptly become the butt of noisy jokes. Eric McCarron, a hard-nosed smart aleck apprentice, had stretched the fun too far and was now suffering Billy's wrath. Pete, in typical fashion, had disappeared at the first sign of trouble, and Phil and others began drifting towards cover.

"All right," Eric was saying, "I just said a pretty Easter bonnet would match your yellow jersey – "

"I heard you the first time, kiddo. And I said a whale's tail would match your mouth."

Billy edged Gobbledegook right alongside Eric's mount, daring him to stand his ground. Eric didn't move. With a provocative grin he said, "Talk about big mouths, you could *swallow* a whale. I'm sorry. In this dim morning light I mistook you for a girl."

Billy went to swipe at him but he manoeuvred away, drawing up his reins.

"Can you ride as well as you cheek?" he shouted.

"Try me!"

By chance they were near the starter mark of the short circuit, both facing up-course. The challenge was thrown down, and accepted. Eric stooped forward and whipped his horse. There was a spray of dirt and he was off. Billy rose and kicked Gobbledegook. The gelding was bursting with energy, begging to go. He charged, hooves scarcely hitting the turf. Billy came out of the saddle and stood high, braced with her calves.

Eric had a head lead, no more. Billy screamed, urging Gobbledegook, throwing her own weight forward. But Eric knew every inch of this track, every muscle of his mount. He stayed low, flowing so smoothly with the rhythm that man and beast appeared as one. He shot clear, but Billy wasn't trailing for long. Although she had only run the circuit once this morning, she had its geography clear in her mind. Eric was over-reaching. They had at least six furlongs to go and his horse was straining already. Gobbledegook, on the other hand, had lots in store. Harrup, watching through the binoculars, might have thought Billy was about to give in.

But all of a sudden she was making ground, slowly but surely. Eric twisted round to see how far away she was and a look of shock swept over his face. The gap was narrowing, narrowing. Billy whispered to Gobbledegook, "*On, boy! On! Go for it, faster!*" The gelding seemed to understand. He speeded up.

There were four furlongs left, three . . . two . . .

They were neck and neck and the finishing line was rushing towards them. But here Eric had the advantage. A trained and frequent rider, he knew how to force that last surge of effort from his mount. Billy sat back at the vital time, a terrible mistake. With no distance to go, Eric slipped ahead, and they crossed the finishing line seconds apart, but Eric the clear winner.

As they pulled in, Billy slid from her horse. She rolled up the sleeves of her jersey. "Get down!" she demanded of Eric.

Eric was happy to stay out of her reach. "I think you cheek better after all," he grinned.

"You cheated. If you didn't have that start on me, I would have won."

"You can shout your mouth off as much as you like. But the fact is I won and you lost." While Billy was boiling with anger Eric was beaming down at her. "If you could only see yourself," he taunted. "You're a prize berk – and a useless jockey."

Billy tried to grab his leg, but Eric began trotting off. "See you again sometime, loser," he shouted gaily. In a black rage Billy kicked the ground.

On the other side of the gallops Harrup put down his binoculars and Pat laughed. "You saw that too?" Harrup said. Pat nodded. "She can ride well enough," the trainer continued. "But she seems more interested in raising waves."

"She's a pushy kid. But I don't suppose you can blame her for it. She knows the disadvantage she's starting with, being a girl."

"Hmph!"

Pat felt a little disappointed, not for himself but for Billy. Harrup's growling sigh seemed to sum up his opinions on girls as apprentices. Things looked bad for Billy – which was a pity, Pat thought, because watching her race indicated her talent all the more.

John Harrup cut in on Pat's thoughts: "Is anyone interested any more in Eeney's progress? Tiny is bringing him down the straight now."

Harrup and Pat turned eagerly. Sure enough, Tiny had Eeney at a steady gallop at last. Harrup put the binoculars back to his eyes and mumbled away to himself. Pat held his breath. Tiny was doing a fair job all right, but the gelding's performance left a lot to be desired. Even Gobbledegook and the horse from Shentons' had run faster.

Tiny reined in and Harrup did not even bother to check the injured leg. With a restless grunt he said, "Yeah, well, get him back to the stables. I'll have a look at the leg there. When you get off the gallops walk him the rest of the way home." Tiny just pulled a face and trotted off. Harrup handed Pat his binoculars. His expression was fierce. "If Vic Favell had seen that he wouldn't enter Eeney for a donkey derby."

"I dunno. At least he ran even-footed. I take encouragement from that."

"Um." Harrup rolled that over in his mind and brightened up a bit. "I suppose we're still in that awkward position of pushing Eeney for the make-or-break challenge. We have to make a decision."

"I'm not with you."

"Well, like you say, he's running even. That's something. But we don't have much time to get him geared up for Worcester. So we'll have to hurry the schedule along. Take a big chance. Establish for definite whether he is or isn't fit enough."

"You mean – ?"

"I'm talking about the work-out with Shentons' Yard tomorrow. I think we'll enter Eeney, have Tiny ride him out.

Let's see the horse pushed to the limit, let's see him gallop."

Pat scratched his chin thoughtfully. "Yes, we need four runners tomorrow. But – "

Harrup wanted no argument. "Fine. We'll run the horses we have out this morning. John here'll be riding, so use the three other lads to make up the group."

"The girl won't like being left out."

"Spin her a story. Tell her she can maybe ride next time."

At that very moment Billy came on the scene. Harrup had not noticed her draw near because his back was turned. But Pat saw her, and knew she had heard the last few exchanges about the work-out with Shentons' Yard.

In spite of the cold Billy was burning after the race and the row with Eric McCarron. There was a knot of tension inside her and she felt ready to explode. What she had just heard helped matters not at all. In a tight controlled voice she said, "I'm sorry for interrupting, Pat, but I saw you talking with Mr Harrup. I thought maybe you were discussing me."

Embarrassed, Harrup fidgeted. "Er, no. Well, yes. We were just saying we'd seen you ride on the far circuit and thought you were . . . well, pretty competent."

Billy caught Pat's eye and looked daggers at him. "Maybe I could have a word with you now, Mr Harrup? About my future here."

Pat took the hint. He crossed to Harrup's son. "Like to stroll down to the stables with me, John? I always walk up here for the leg stretch. Does me good. And you could do with the exercise . . ."

When they had gone Billy stood facing Harrup. She was too wound up to be nervous. "I understand you've been busy, Mr Harrup, but I must talk to you about my job. You see, like I said, I'm only here because I want an apprenticeship. I want to be a jockey. When we spoke in London you told me that was the kind of opening I could expect at a racing stables."

"I said that?" Harrup shook his head. "No, I don't think I

41

did. You asked me was it true that most lads joined up and worked through to become apprentices. I said yes. I didn't promise anything. I took you on because you seemed intelligent, reasonable and enthusiastic – "

"I remember it different," Billy insisted. "Anyway, you see I can ride, I can race. Why can't I have the chances the others have?"

"All right, all right. Don't go off the deep end. There's no room in racing for anyone with a temper like yours – so just try and control yourself!"

Billy's flaring fury died and Harrup stood muttering to himself, as though counting quietly to ten. Satisfied by the silence, Harrup started again, "Right. The situation as far as all of my lads are concerned is that they must go on a month's trial for their apprenticeship. So – after a month we'll look at things again. OK?"

"What does that mean? You'll give me an apprenticeship after a month?"

Harrup wasn't sure he wanted to answer that one. He raised his big shoulders in a vague gesture. "Maybe, if you're good enough – "

"But you already said I rode well. Why – ?"

"Please!" Harrup was beginning to lose his grip on *his* temper. "I said we'll see after a month. Right? I want to see how you ride different mounts in different conditions. Also whether you fit in here." He could see by her expression that Billy was ready to back down and he took advantage. "Now, we haven't had much chance to talk about basics. So let's square it here and now. You're on what the other lads are getting – forty pounds a week, less twenty for your keep. After deductions that'll leave you with sixteen pounds . . ."

Billy was half-listening. Harrup was side-stepping again. He was giving no guarantees. Maybe, in the long run, he had no intention of allowing her the jockey stakes. Suddenly he prodded her arm. "Are you listening, girl? What's up now, for heaven's sake?"

42

Billy shrugged. "Why am I left out tomorrow? I overheard some of that talk with Pat."

Harrup cleared his throat and plucked at his soft hat. "Well, it's a simple matter of running only four horses. I must give the rides to the four that were here first. That's only fair."

"But it's not. They have their apprenticeships."

"Just because they have doesn't mean they're not looking for new experiences, new rides."

"But I can't win then, can I? How can I prove myself to you unless I have the opportunity to race?"

The conversation was turning like a wheel going nowhere and Harrup's patience was gone. "This is pointless," he said severely. "I think we have covered everything we need to, Billy. You applied for a job as stables help and I've offered it. You know the score, you're sensible enough. Now if you don't like it, you can pack your case this afternoon and head back to Burnham." He didn't wait for a response but turned and climbed into the Landrover.

Billy patted Gobbledegook and watched as the car spun round on the gravel and made for the village road. She felt upset rather than angry. There was no time for anger. The last thing in the world she intended to do was pack her bags. Girls, her dear Mum used to say, had a gift over boys – and that was wiliness. There and then she decided to *prove* her talent, beyond doubt, to Harrup. She would show him she was not only a good rider, but potentially the best he had. And she wouldn't wait a month for the proof. She would show him soon. Sooner than he thought.

\*

Sparsholt village was not without its attractions, but nearby Lambourn had the pubs and cafes that attracted racing folk enjoying their free time. *The King's Cup* was one of the most popular pubs. Every night droves of people came from the different stables and the uninformed visitor was often startled to find a bar chock-full of what appeared to be under-age drinkers. In fact, most of the pint-size customers were apprentices of proper age, or qualified jockeys.

On Thursday nights, by custom, the lads of Rectory Stables hitched into Lambourn to enjoy their midweek night off. Tiny was under age but, accompanied by Pete and manly-looking Phil and under cover of the teeming masses, they had no trouble joining the fun of *The King's Cup*. Billy was determined not to be left out, even though being a girl "lad", she naturally drew attention to herself. Tiny and Pete seemed a little warmer towards her, and with their support she joined the party.

In the pub they got an alcove table and while Phil went for drinks they chatted. Pete as usual had little to say, but Tiny unwittingly explained their change of attitude towards her. Word of her ambition was out – thanks to Pat probably. Clearly the lads admired her pluck, but felt sorry for her. They did not say it, but Billy knew they held no hope for her. Since the cards were on the table she decided to come clean and tell all. She told of her encounters with Harrup and his roundabout answers to her questions. And she emphasised her determination to win through.

Phil returned with the drinks and Billy voiced her annoyance about the inter-stables work-out. Everyone was surprised by the urgency of her ambition. "I wouldn't get het up about that were I you," Tiny said. Rather limply he added: "At least Dobbin hasn't told you to get lost. He's prepared in principle to give you a month's trial – or so he says."

Phil gave a short laugh of disbelief. "You must understand that there are very, very few girl jockeys. And fewer good ones. By and large men *race* better – "

"By and large – that may be. But I'm different. I can handle horses. All I need is the chance to show Harrup that I *could be* really good." Billy gave an exasperated sigh. "I

44

mean, why can't he throw me in the deep end? Why can't he run five horses in the work-out?"

"Whew!" Phil whistled low. "Next you'll be asking Dobbin to rearrange the schedules to suit you!" He leant forward to drive his point home. "Don't you understand that you were employed because the stables needed a help-out? There are too many horses to be tended by us alone. We badly needed some extra muscle."

Tiny saw Billy's frustrated grimace and stepped helpfully into the breach. "Anyway, if Dobbin means what he says there'll be other work-outs."

"How often do they happen?" Billy asked.

"Oh, half-a-dozen times a year."

"See, that's what I mean! If I don't get a chance tomorrow I'll have to wait for weeks and weeks. I'm not having that, no way."

There was something in Billy's voice that stunned the conversation to silence. Pete wasn't much bothered, moodily gazing into his drink. But Phil and Tiny stared expectantly. At length Tiny asked, "What are you going to do then? Try some trick to get in on the action tomorrow?"

"Yes, if I have to."

"Like what? Sabotage us? Knock me or Phil over the head?"

Many loosely-formed ideas had been floating through Billy's head. But what Tiny had just said sparked off a new idea. Billy's fist pounded the table top. Her eyes lit up. "Tiny, you've hit on it. That's it! That's my way of showing Harrup."

"Wha – ?" Phil and Tiny looked at each other.

"Don't you see?" she laughed. "What a trick! I can pretend I'm one of you."

Phil mumbled, "You're out of your mind."

Billy was bouncing with excitement in her chair. "It would be simple. I could dress up in one of your clothes. If Harrup stands with the spectators on the gravel pitch, he'd never cop me." She grabbed Phil's arm. "How about it? You've been under the weather. You don't want to have to sweat it out tomorrow."

Phil was lost for words but Tiny said: "She thinks it's a flippin' pantomime."

Billy showed her teeth. "Don't be so mean. Why not give me a break? After the gallop it could be easily explained away. No one would get into trouble."

"Don't look at me," Tiny said. "It's tough that you're in such a hurry, but I can't help. Do you realise I've taken a cut in wages to get more rides? You don't know how Dobbin can be, he's so mean. And I need all the rides I can get if I want an apprenticeship."

She swung back on Phil. "All right then – Phil. Please – ?"

Pete stood up, seemingly indifferent to the whole conversation. "I'll fetch some more drinks." When he'd moved off Phil made it clear in no uncertain terms that, cold or not, he would be riding tomorrow.

The cross-talk went on for another hour, and even when they left the pub and began hitching back to Sparsholt, Billy's pleading persisted. They had skipped dinner but, as was usual for Thursdays, joined Una and Pat in their bungalow for supper. Here the chat was light and sociable and Billy was forced to surrender. After a while she fell in to a gloomy huff while Pat, Una and the boys nattered about Ascot, the National and great races of old. Pete had excused himself early but everyone started to turn for bed at eleven-thirty. Billy was on her way to the door when Una reminded her that it was her turn to assist with the washing-up. Depressed, Billy dragged her heels towards the kitchen.

Una was a brisk, open Londoner with smiling eyes. There was nothing of the frilly doll-like femininity about her that Billy so disliked, but her clothes were fashionable and her manners perfect. Pat loved her dearly, the boys respected her and indeed Billy liked her – though she had reservations about those painted fingernails! Billy had never bothered much with nail varnish and make-up. While the girls back home experimented with new mascara and new boyfriends, Billy had contented herself with reading and the farm work.

As they worked side by side Una told Billy how impressed Pat had been by her morning ride. Billy hardly listened. She was working so fast and carelessly that it seemed inevitable she would drop and break one of the dishes she was drying. "Steady on," Una said. "What's the big rush?"

"Uh, nothin'. I just kind of work fast."

Una wasn't convinced. "Whatever it is, it will wait." She watched as Billy obediently dried with more care. She thought she understood Billy's bad mood. "You set high standards for yourself, Billy," she said. "Is your Dad in the racing business?"

Billy smiled for the first time in three hours. "I suppose he is in a way. He keeps the betting shops going." Una laughed and Billy explained, "He works in a bakery actually."

"So where does this crazy obsession for horses come from?"

"I don't know." Billy's face screwed into a funny, thoughtful mask. "I've always loved animals, of course. But it's more than that. From very early on I wanted to combine a career with animals and a competitive-type career. I always loved races. Kids running races, horses racing on telly. You know. I think . . ." She blushed a little at the seriousness of her tone. "I grew up among men. Brothers, Dad, uncles. I was always given the chores to do, but never the chance to be *myself*, if you know what I mean. I made the tea and made the beds and all . . . but I never got noticed. I was never anybody, just a help. Well, I reckoned I was as good as any man. And I wanted to compete in something and prove it."

Billy's voice was fading with embarrassment. Una cut in: "I think I understand. Now you're away from home at last and the world is open to you?"

Billy sighed. "Open? I wish it was."

47

"Be patient. Take your time. Wait for your luck, it'll come."

"Me Mum used to say you make your own luck."

The last plates were dried and Una rinsed the sink. "That wasn't too bad, was it? Five minutes and we even had a chance to chat. It's nice to talk out your thoughts at times."

Billy towelled her hands. "I'm sorry if I was a bit, well, glum tonight. It's just that, er – "

"That you've got important things on your mind. Things that you're rushing off to settle now?" Una pressed Billy's hand in a comforting way. "Remember what I said: that it's good to discuss things before flying off the handle. So if you ever want a sympathetic ear, you know where to come."

"Thanks, I'll remember." Billy trusted Una, but understood her loyalty to Pat, and to the boss. It would be unwise to confide too much just now. Saying goodnight, Billy left the bungalow. The plan triggered by Tiny in *The King's Cup* was still rattling through her head and she was eager to make one last attempt at persuasion. Phil wouldn't budge and Tiny genuinely needed the ride. But what of quiet Pete? In the pub, on the way back, his reactions had been strangely vague. Perhaps if she could talk to him once more, maybe alone. Maybe if she promised him a fiver from her pay packet . . .?

Moving towards the hostel Billy suddenly saw a light burning in the stable. She automatically walked over to check it out.

At first there seemed to be no one in the big stable – then she saw a dark head pop up above a far stall. She sauntered quietly down and found Pete gently grooming Domino. "Hey," she said in amazement, "don't you ever get enough of horses? It's nearly midnight."

Pete brushed Domino's ears and shrugged.

"So this is where you get to late at nights?" Billy continued.

"Sometimes. More fun than the hostel, I guess."

48

"I take your point," she said boldly. She watched Pete give a sugar lump to the horse and pat it fondly. "You really love horses, don't you? And you're a good rider."

He moved his shoulders. "Don't much care whether I'm good or not. I don't really *try*. It's the horses I love, not the racing . . ."

Billy saw her opening. "I love the horses too, Pete. But I want to race, I want to *win*. I know it might *seem* greedy but . . . I really can't wait. I want my apprenticeship. Tomorrow I have a chance."

Pete fed Domino another piece of sugar. "You want *me* to slip away while you take my place for the race?"

"Please, Pete." She felt like screaming it.

Without a flicker of an eye, totally unexpectedly, he said, "Yeah, all right."

# FOUR

Even though the meetings with other yards were only friendly, there was always an air of high tension about them. This morning was worse than usual because of the make-or-break test that Eeney faced. From the moment Pat showed his face after breakfast everyone knew he was extra-anxious. So there were grim faces all round.

By eight o'clock the groups had begun to assemble at the gallops. The chosen run was at the edge of the gallops and on a lower level from the main run. Here the four riders from Shentons' Stables met the team from Rectory. Having dropped off Harrup at the gravel pitch, Pat motored down to line up the runners. Una sat with him in the Landrover but thought it better not to speak. When Pat pulled up he immediately saw that something was amiss. He checked his list of runners and beckoned to Tiny.

"Where's Pete? What's the hold-up? I saw Gobbledegook saddled and ready when I was leaving the yard."

"There was some small delay, Pat. Pete was in the hostel when we moved out, but I called to him and he said he'd be after us in five minutes."

Pat grunted. "Well, he'd better shake a leg. Anyway, it's lucky he's running last."

Tiny craned down. "Where's the guv'nor?" he whispered.

"Chatting with Reggie Shenton up on the pitch. Exchanging their bets, no doubt." Pat cast a critical eye over Eeney.

"How does he seem this morning? Stiff?"

"Not really. I'm surprised. The rest yesterday after the exercise seems to have loosened 'im up a lot."

"Well, let's keep our fingers crossed."

A peppy voice suddenly called out, "Who's off first, chief? We're on starting time." Pat turned to see Eric McCarron mounted on Royal Victor, one of Shentons' best hopes. The cheeky face registered complete confidence.

"You'll have to wait your turn, I'm afraid. First is The Najes from your stable versus Lady Laughter." John Harrup on Lady Laughter spurred his horse up to the starting line. He looked quite happy, and understandably so. The Najes was nearly two years older than Lady Laughter, which had two seasons of poor form behind her. The odds were in favour of Rectory to begin with. The Shentons' boys stirred uneasily while The Najes took her mark.

"What's up with your side?" Eric went on sarcastically. "Can you only dig up three horses worth racing?"

Pat ignored the remark but Tiny came back: "We'd only need *one* horse to take on your rubbish."

"All right, no nonsense now." Pat moved into position at the starter mark. In the distance he could see the band of spectators on the high pitch, Harrup conspicuously to the fore. He wondered briefly whether the guv'nor was feeling as jumpy as he was.

On the gravel pitch Reggie Shenton's chat was keeping Harrup occupied. Shenton was in his late forties, one of the gentlemen-farmer type trainers rather than ex-jockey types. He was easy-going and slow-voiced, the kind of man with whom one could easily be frank. Harrup had candidly admitted that things could be running smoother at his stables and Shenton was consoling him.

"Well, Jack, we're all suffering the pinch. To tell you the truth I'm having to dip into my own pocket to bale out the stabling side."

"No problem to you though, Reggie. You've got a second

string to your bow with the farm. I've just got the stables."

"True enough. Still – you might do yourself a bit of good here today, eh? Who's first? Looks like The Najes and . . . yes, Lady Laughter I believe. How'll we start the betting? Nice 'n easy for openers?"

Harrup remembered that his son was riding Lady Laughter. That didn't necessarily lessen the filly's chances, but . . . "Make it a fiver to begin with," he suggested cautiously.

They could see Pat Devlin's arm going up at the starting line. Shenton said, "A fiver? That's a bit pessimistic, isn't it? But – suits me." He was privately breathing relief, recalling The Najes' form.

"There they go!" Somebody let out a cheer.

John was a bad rider, excited when he should have sat back, too relaxed at the vital times. The Najes did very badly and yet, with the final furlong to go, there were only a few lengths between the horses. Lady Laughter tired a bit and Shenton clapped his hands, thinking he had it. John was sitting back, coasting Lady Laughter when he should have been giving her a touch of the whip. Harrup shouted out, urging him on. For a few seconds it looked positively as if his fiver had gone. Then The Najes fell suddenly back, exhausted.

Lady Laughter crossed the line a good length or two ahead of its rival.

"Yours," Shenton snapped. He pounded a fist into his open palm. "Oh well, early days yet I suppose. Some of my better things have yet to come. Now, let's see." He found a crumpled copy of the running order in his overcoat pocket and consulted it. A frown ruckled his brow. "Ho, well, here's an interesting challenge! My Stony Ground against your Eeney. Two champs – this should jangle the nerves a bit, what?"

Harrup merely sucked air. The hand that held his binoculars was wet with sweat. "Should be fun," he said shortly.

"What bet?"

"Er, fiver again?"

Shenton's thick eyebrows zoomed. "Come now, you're letting me get away with murder, Jack. A fiver on Eeney! I know Stony Ground's good, but Eeney is coming to his peak, no doubt about it." Harrup's face was blank and Shenton stopped abruptly and decided to keep his thoughts to himself. Business must be pretty shaky indeed at Rectory for old Harrup to be keeping his hand on his wallet. "A fiver it is, then," he said. Under his breath he mumbled, "But I reckon it's going to be another fiver up to you, old son."

Harrup took the binoculars and focused on the gelding's legs. Was he trembling with tension, or the cold?

Down at the starting line Pat was whispering final instructions to Tiny. "You've been on Eeney before, you know the score. Let Stony Ground make the running – but push him before the home. Don't rely on him to make up lost ground on the final furlong . . ."

Tiny's nerves had suddenly got the better of him. "I wish you'd let Phil have this 'un, Pat. He's more experienced and he knows Eeney better."

"You know what you're doing," Pat said confidently. "You're a good rider and you need to ride different horses if you're to make that apprenticeship. Anyway, seems to me Phil's glad to be free of the responsibility here."

"Yeah, I can believe that." Tiny turned and winked at Phil who gave a rueful grin and a thumbs up.

"Ready?" Pat shouted as he stood back and lifted his arm. Both riders nodded. Stony Ground and Eeney stood dead still. "Off!" Pat dropped his arm and the horses bolted as though startled by thunder. Before they were five seconds away Pat was up on the bonnet of the Landrover beside Una, standing straight as a ramrod. From there they had a clear view of Eeney's progress.

The horses were running neck-and-neck, then Eeney seemed to stumble. For a terrible moment Pat thought he was going to fall. Una gripped his arm. She was no expert, but she had a good, trained eye. "He shouldn't be running really, Pat," she said.

"Try telling that to Harrup." Pat leaned forward.

"But why is he doing it if Eeney's got a bad leg?" Una persisted.

"Sssh! Don't tell the world," said Pat. "The guv'nor's trying to get himself out of a corner."

"So what's new about that?" mumbled Una under her breath, switching her attention to the horses.

Eeney had recovered from the stumble, and she saw Tiny give him a touch of the whip. But it was too late – Eeney's drive had gone. Stony Ground simply could not be caught. Tiny was terrified. He knew Eeney would fall if this pace was kept up. But what could he do? He had been ordered to gallop him, not jaunt him out. Tiny closed his mind. He refused to think what a fall might do to that dicey leg.

Up on the gravel pitch Reggie Shenton was gazing down in wonder. He knew Stony Ground would make a good go of it against Eeney, but he hadn't expected this. Eeney had never really taken off. Maybe it wasn't the horse, but that new young lad? He said to Harrup, "You've obviously got your reasons for only putting a fiver on Eeney."

Beside him Harrup had gone white. Stuffing his binoculars into his pocket he hurried away from Shenton and down the slope towards the final furlong. As he neared the bottom Stony Ground flashed by and, seconds later, Eeney approached. "Pull 'im up!" Harrup shouted to Tiny. "Stop now!"

Through the sweat in his eyes, Tiny caught the glimpse of Harrup and recognised the frantic gestures. He tore in the reins and nursed the gelding down.

Harrup rushed up. Tiny said thankfully, apologetically: "He's not himself at all, guv'nor. He's got no zip in him."

"Get him back to the stables. Make him comfortable and I'll check him over when I get there."

"I'm sorry about the way it went – "

Harrup brushed that aside. "Not your fault, no one's fault. That's the way it goes. Take him home now."

Harrup signalled the stopping of the gallop to Pat Devlin and stalked up to the spectators' pitch in foul humour. Shenton looked mildly shocked. "Eeney all right, is he?"

"Sure, sure. Just didn't want to force him. He might be sickening for a cold. The lad said he was coughing on the way up. Give 'im a day or two and he'll be right as rain."

"Too bad about your fiver. But that squares us." Shenton watched the action at the starting line. Pat was already lining up the next pair – Domino, ridden by Phil, and Falcon Tony, a temperamental three-year-old. The outcome was anybody's guess but Shenton's faith in his own team suddenly soared. It seemed to him Jack Harrup was running a lot of ill-prepared outsiders. No more fivers, here was the time to make a little drinking money on a decent bet. "Let's be a bit adventurous, Jack. Let's say twenty-five quid on this, eh?"

Harrup was in no mood to squabble. He muttered a "yes" and was about to fix his binoculars when, from the tail of his eye, he saw a horse plodding up the pathway that led from the village road, coming in his direction. His eyes widened. Gobbledegook was heading for the high gallops, with the figure of Pete in the saddle.

"Where d'you think you're going?" Harrup called out. "They're waiting for you at the seven furlong mark. I can see Pat in a tizzy. Get down there!"

The approaching rider nearly tumbled from the saddle in fright. The horse was swiftly pulled up.

"Did you hear me?" Harrup barked. "I said, hurry up."

Billy, dressed as Pete, gave a curt wave. Her heart was slamming. It was incredible that Harrup had not recognised her at this short range. True, she had taken every precaution. Her hair was pinned tightly up under Pete's customary tatty black helmet and she was wearing his Aran jersey and black jodhpurs. But the intention was to deceive the eye at reasonably *long* range. She had assumed the gallops would happen on the high run, and had been carefully picking a path towards it. She had not anticipated finding Harrup and the spectators on *this* end of the gravel pitch, facing *this* direction.

Now, somewhat behind schedule, she had to make tracks fast for the lower run. The success of the venture, in her mind, depended solely on good timing. And, as it happened, her timing could not have been better. The third race was dashing through its final stage. Domino and Falcon Tony were neck and neck and everybody's attention was on them. Only Eric McCarron turned to acknowledge her arrival, but he didn't seem to recognise her either. He went back to watching the end of the race. So the disguise must be good, Billy thought.

A distant small cheer rang out as Domino crossed the finishing line lengths ahead of the Shentons' horse. Eric's face fell; Pat and Una clapped. But Billy could tell from their expressions that not everything had gone so well. She gave a deep, nervous sigh. This was perhaps not the best time to try the trick and show her hand – but she had no choice.

As Domino and Falcon Tony cantered away into the distance, unwinding, Pat read out from his list: "Last run. Royal Victor and Gobbledegook." Remembering that Pete had been missing he glanced quickly round. "Pete? Ha, good. You've arrived." He walked over casually, his attention now on the gravel spectators' pitch. Almost to himself he said, "You missed Eeney, I suppose? Well, it turned out rotten. The guv'nor pulled him up. We'll have to wait till we get back and – " Suddenly he saw who he was speaking to. He looked puzzled, then angry. "What the hell are you doing here!"

"Standing in for Pete."

"What's wrong with him? Have you been . . . getting at him?" His eyes were raking over her clothes, confused.

"He had a stomach-ache, Pat. Really he did."

Royal Victor was at the starting line a bit away but Pat quickly decided: "You can get down, Billy. You're not riding." She tried to cut in but he wouldn't let her: "You're not riding because I've heard about the kind of games you wanted to play and I'm not prepared to stand here and let you manipulate all of us for your own aims. . . ."

"But, Pat . . ." She had not expected this harsh resistance, nor the black look in Pat's eye. She searched for words, but could only go back to lying: "I'm only standing in for a rider who can't make it."

"So you say. I see things differently, I'm afraid."

At that moment Una interrupted. She had overheard the argument but kept apart from it. Now she pulled Pat to one side. Royal Victor was getting restless and Eric shouted something impatiently. "You might be wrong about Billy," Una told her husband. "But even if she has talked Pete out of his ride she's here now. You might as well let her have her chance." Pat mulled over that while Eric called out again. "Besides," Una urged, "it's not going to look good if you withdraw one of your rides. We haven't exactly scored this morning. Lady Laughter didn't do well; Eeney was a disaster. And Domino only came through because Phil had the edge of experience over that apprentice from Shentons', to my thinking. If you withdraw the last horse it'll be one up for Reggie Shenton."

Pat turned away from Una. She didn't need to force the point: everything she said was true. Pulling out Gobbledegook now would be like admitting to another dud after Eeney. He said to Billy, gruffly, "All right, you can ride. Get up to your starter."

He followed Gobbledegook up to the line. Eric was smirking. " 'Bout time. I thought you were writing yer life stories." Then he recoiled, suddenly noticing the familiar face of his rival, remembering yesterday. He went slightly pale. "Hey, what's this? No one said – ?"

"Change of rider," Pat explained. "The lad who was due up wasn't well. This is our replacement, if that's all right with you?" Pat too was recalling the unscheduled race between this pair on the far circuit. Word had come back to him that it had been accompanied by a bitter slanging match.

But Eric was not about to bow before the girl. Boldly he grinned, "Suits me. I wiped her out before, I can do it again."

"You'd want to watch that," Billy needled. "Insanity is taking a hold of you."

"I want none of this," Pat demanded. "A clean fair run – OK? Act your age."

Billy shook her head to clear her concentration. So – she had made it this far. Even if Dobbin recognised her through the binoculars now it was too late. Pat was readying himself for the *go* sign. Her chance was at hand. Gobbledegook stirred under her and she had the inevitable last-minute qualms. She did not know the horse, knew only his reputation. *Just ride him hard*, Pete had said; *he won't tire over that distance*. Billy was suddenly uncertain of herself, and the horse. She had no way of knowing that, just then, Harrup was not sharing her lack of confidence. Having scooped twenty-five quid with Domino, thanks to Phil's expertise, he was now putting that "take" back down on Pete. Fighting through his depression he told Reggie Shenton arrogantly that Gobbledegook would walk it!

Pat's hand went up. But before it fell for the starting signal, Royal Victor burst forward like a bat out of hell.

"Cheat!" Billy swore to herself, as she prodded Gobblelegook's sides and urged him forward. By the time a furlong had been run, she was equal with Royal Victor.

"You cheated!' she shouted furiously.

"I don't need to cheat against you, girly," Eric smirked.

"What did you do back at the start then? You can't win without cheating!"

"Watch this then!" Eric gave his horse a touch of the stick and Royal Victor began to gain.

Furious, Billy dug in her heels and urged Gobbledegook on until they were side by side. "So what am I supposed to be watching then?" she demanded, murder in her eyes.

Eric was angry. He had expected an easy victory. Now he urged Royal Victor into the side, leaning on Gobbledegook, forcing Billy into the rough grass at the side of the run. Furiously, shouting at Eric, she managed to pull back on course and bring Gobbledegook level again. In her temper she hardly realised what she was doing as she tried the same tactic. Urging, whispering, talking to Gobbledegook, she leaned into Eric's path, forcing him towards the fence on the far side, then galloped triumphantly on. She was past and away before she realised anything was wrong. Royal Victor, all of a sudden, was gone.

Billy didn't pull back. She kept Gobbledegook charging, but glanced over her shoulder. Amazingly, Eric fluffed it in the worst possible way. He had run Royal Victor *into* the fence. The horse looked to be all right, but Eric had taken quite a fall. He was lying in a heap in the muck at the trackside. Billy smiled to herself, then turned back to the job before her. She slapped Gobbledegook on. She had it! She saw it as a race, and it was hers. A first, sweet victory at a small but important event. *Hers.*

Gobbledegook performed exquisitely over the remainder of the course and Billy crossed the finishing line singing to herself. As they slowed to a trot the breeze died around her ears and, in a split second it seemed, the world was deathly silent. Billy was fainly surprised. Somehow she had expected – *something!* A whistling call of congratulations, a few hand claps . . .

There was no one at all near the finishing line and she glanced behind her. Everyone was crowding around the figure crumpled up beside the track. The Landrover was just arriving and she could see Shenton and Una half-carry Eric inside.

Billy rode down the course as the crowd started to break up and the Landrover prepared to move off. Harrup marched smartly towards her. They met some distance away from the scene of the mishap. His face was pinched and pale. "I have to see it with my own eyes," he said. "I knew it couldn't be Pete who'd behave like that. When Pat told me it was you – " He shook his head in dismay.

"Is . . . is he all right?"

"We think so. He's probably concussed, not dangerously. But it's as well to have these things checked. You know, that lad could've been badly injured because of what you did."

Billy felt she was treading thin ice. "But he did it to me first. What am I supposed to do? Just let him push me into the side and smile?"

"You didn't have to push him into a fence," Harrup said firmly. "What kind of pickle would I have been in if the horse was damaged?"

"Well, he could've damaged Gobbledegook when he pushed me out!"

"You've got more excuses than a leopard's got spots!" Harrup exploded. "You should have stopped and given the lad a hand."

"Why? I only did to him what he did to me. And I won the race."

"This was a friendly gallop, not a real race."

"They're the same, ain't they?"

"No."

"It was a race and I won . . ." Billy's gall was rising. "That's what it's all about as far as I'm concerned."

Harrup ground his teeth. "There are things to learn about racing besides winning. You behaved badly, and that's just as important."

"But you see now I can ride well in competition. If you give me my apprenticeship – "

"Your apprenticeship just like that!" Harrup almost laughed the words. But his expression was grave. "I think I can put two and two together and tell what's happened here today. You think you've achieved something by running today, eh? Well, you've achieved something all right. You've proved to me just how unready you are for an apprenticeship.

You're immature, thoughtless and too big for your boots. A jockey must be caring and patient."

"But I just want – "

"We all just want. Learn to work. And wait, Billy. Otherwise you're out on your ear. Today!" And he strode away.

Billy fought back a tear. Immature, thoughtless . . .? Yes, she felt all those things – and a little stupid besides. She hoped Eric would be all right. Deep down she did care about those things. She was only human. But a career mattered too. Why couldn't anyone recognise her talents?

She thought back to Burnham, to the years of chores, of coping with her young brothers. The dreams of independence and a career kept her sane then. And yet here she was free, and out in the wild world: and every door seemed closed to her. She wondered, for the thousandth time, whether dreams really ever do come true.

# FIVE

It was mid-day when Pat and Harrup got together to check Eeney's leg. Pat had been delayed at Shentons' where he'd hung around to hear the doctor's report on Eric. "The kid was OK," he explained to Harrup. "Just a bit dazed and bruised around the neck. Doc says he was lucky not to cop one of the jockey's old reliables – broken collar-bone."

"Royal Victor all right?"

Pat nodded and crouched beside Harrup. "What about this fella?" As Pat spoke, trouble was looking him in the eye. Eeney. At neck and flanks Eeney's bay hide was blotched with sweat. The injured leg had taken a lot of bashing and was swollen and hot. Not only that. The off-hind appeared to be tender too, where the hoof had hit a fence bar.

Harrup had already taken all this in and was gazing abstractedly into mid-air. There were six days to Worcester and he was working out his chances. Pat, beside him, needed no time to make up his mind. After this morning Eeney would need to rest up for quite a while. He certainly wouldn't be up to training on the gallops tomorrow morning. "I think," Pat said carefully, "any kind of decent preparation programme is gone out the window, guv'nor."

There was a loaded pause, then Harrup said in an airy burst, "I've been trying to figure out what to do, Pat. The way it stands *I* lose whatever happens now. If I don't run him at Worcester, Favell withdraws him from here. If I do he'll lose – and Favell will withdraw him as well."

"So, what's to be done? If we try to force a training schedule –"

"No. The animal isn't well enough. I'm going to rest him up, then run him as planned. Stone cold."

Pat clucked unhappily. "I know Worcester isn't the toughest set-up and the field won't be that exciting but, other things considered, it seems to me Eeney hasn't a hope of winning."

"Uh-huh, I accept that." Harrup's eyes narrowed and his face became sly. "However, there's an emergency plan in the back of my mind that just might save us."

Pat didn't like the sound of that at all. He studied his boss's expression. "Since you say yourself you can't win, what possible plan might change that?"

"I need to talk to Vic Favell," Harrup said quietly. "And a few other people." Before Pat could pursue his questions, Harrup bluntly changed the subject: "What about that girl Billy? Is she too much trouble to hold on to? You're my sounding machine, Pat. Just say the word and she's gone."

Pat took a minute to get his bearings. Una had told him a thing or two about Billy's background, and her ambition, on the way back to the stables. The annoyance he had felt about the trick she'd pulled had passed. And, he reminded himself, she showed potential. "Give her a little more elbow room, I reckon. I may be wrong, but a couple of things said to her in the last few days might wise her up a bit."

"I hope you're right. There's problems I have to put up with, but there's plenty I can do without . . ."

Phil had entered the big stable. "Just thought you'd like to know, guv'nor. Vic Favell's car's driving up."

"No, not now!" Harrup crashed into a dither. "Dammit. All right, Phil, get about your normal duties. You too, Pat. Don't make any big scene in here with Eeney. Oh, and Phil – get that Billy. Tell her to keep her face out of sight while Favell's around. Where is she?"

"Dunno, but I'll find out." Phil skipped off. He had picked

63

up the full story about Billy's insulting Favell and understood the emergency.

Vic Favell came straight into the stable, hurrying as though chasing the clock. Before confronting Harrup he looked purposefully in on his few horses.

"Dropped by because I hadn't heard from you, Jack," Favell said. "We're a few days nearer to Worcester and I want to know how Eeney's progressing. Form good?"

They were standing near the gelding's stall, but Favell had yet to see more than Eeney's head. Harrup was blocking his path.

Harrup took a deep breath before he launched into it. He knew he had no options: the truth must be told. "I'm, er, glad you came by, Mr Favell. I was about to phone you anyway. You see, there's something you should know . . ."

Favell flinched as though struck a blow. He read everything in his trainer's face. "Good Lord, man. There's something wrong. Eeney's not fit?"

"Not exactly fit, no. Y'see . . . well, let's not beat about the bush. The gelding sustained a leg injury – a minor one, mind – at Sandown. I've done what I could, but it's unlikely to get better in time for next week's race."

Favell's face burned red. "Let me see!" He swept past Harrup and into the stall. He glanced over the leg, then staggered back, aghast. "You idiot, Harrup. How in heaven's name . . .!" He lit a cigar fast, greedily sucking it, calming himself. "Why didn't you tell me about this before?"

"Let's be fair, er . . ." Harrup chanced the intimacy. "Let's be fair, Vic. Last time we talked you were in no mood to listen."

"That was mainly the fault of that stupid girl you had here."

Harrup kept his impassive gaze. "You see, it's never easy to break the true facts to an owner. If I'd said the gelding damaged his leg because he ran on the soft at Sandown you'd probably have denied that was the cause."

"Well, I'm not sure it is!"

"There you are. Owners always want to believe their horses are infallible. But Sandown was wrong for Eeney."

For a full minute Favell said nothing, just steamed away. "So Eeney won't be fit enough to run at Worcester?" he growled at last.

"I didn't say that. I said his leg won't get better. He won't win."

"Same difference to me, Jack. I told you I need a bit of cash. I needed to back him heavily and get myself out of trouble. But if he's not going to win I stay in the same boat."

Harrup chewed his lip. This was it, this was where he risked outrage, risked a slur on his reputation. "There are circumstances where you can win when you lose. And the, er, conditions are right in this case."

"I see." Favell's eyes were as keen as a fox's. "What you're saying . . . is this illegal?"

"Not strictly speaking, I'm sure."

"How much is there in it?"

"If he was racing to win what would your bet have been on him?"

"I would've been looking to win around two thousand."

"Well, there'll probably be a bit more than that in it."

"More – for losing?" Favell banged a fist against the side of his head as if trying to get his brain functioning faster. "It sounds crazy. Are you sure you can work it?"

"It can't be done without involving a bookie. But there's one I know who should be interested. If you wait till I see him, wait till he says he'll come in with us, then I'll tell you what the scheme is."

Favell shrugged his well-clad shoulders. "Fair enough, I suppose." The words were out before he knew he'd said them.

"As long as I know that you agree to the deal I can start arranging it. It's going to have to be split fifty-fifty between us and the bookie. I'll just take ten per cent of our share for arranging it . . ." Harrup paused for emphasis: "As long as it's agreed you continue to stable your horses here."

Favell was already trapped, lost. "Agreed."

Harrup led him towards the door. "Good, then let's have a drink on it over at the house."

At the very moment Harrup was reaching to open the stable door, across the yard – in clear sight from the stable once the door opened – Billy was ambling from the storage shed. She had been moping about in the hostel since morning and only just begun work again. As she stepped from the shed a tough hand gripped her forearm and tugged viciously. She went to scream with fright but a hand suddenly cupped her mouth. She was pulled back into the shadows. "Hush up," a voice hissed as she was pressed against the wall. "Can't you see whose car that is! The boss says you'd best lie low while Favell's around."

Through the crack in the door they saw Harrup and Favell stride towards the big Georgian house. Billy relaxed, understanding. But Phil did not let her go. She tried to shrug him off but the grip was like a vice. His eyes blazed. "Pretty rotten, isn't it," he sneered, "having to hide in the dark like a criminal – all because your filthy manners offended someone."

"Let me worry for myself," Billy retorted. "And kindly let me go. I know the situation with Mr Favell exactly, thank you, and it's none of your business . . ."

"Your behaviour is beginning to be all our business, Billy."

"What's that supposed to mean?" She wormed out of his hands at last, but stood frostily, ready for fight.

"I don't think you understand the value of friendships, or the process of making friends. You think you can do everything by yourself." He thought for a moment, then changed tracks. "I just want to let you know we all think you took a hell of a liberty with Pete. He was the weak link, always is. He's the one anyone can talk around 'cause he'd do anything to avoid hassle. You spotted that and worked on it – and we don't admire you for it. We've all got ambition and, if we're in the jockey stakes, we need rides. Pete's good, but he hasn't been in competition for a bit and he needed that work-out today – "

Billy was embarrassed and knew that Phil was right, but she tried to conceal it. "Big deal. He missed one ride! No doubt there'll be hundreds of others for him. Anyhow, he didn't mind one bit."

"He wouldn't say if he did. He's a softie behind it all, you see. But he's our friend and we'll defend his interests. He has the chance to be a great jockey, he deserves encouragement."

"Hmph! And I'm nothing of course. Just a girl. Somebody to snigger about and push around."

"If you behave the way you do, that's what you deserve. You push, and we'll push back." Favell and Harrup had disappeared into the house now. Phil shook the dust of the shed off his sleeves and walked to the door. He turned before leaving. "I know it's been hard on you starting here as a girl. Just like it'd be hard for a boy starting in a ballet school, I suppose. But you *are* getting the opportunity to prove yourself, and win our respect. Even if you don't think so. But you're failing, Billy. Failing badly. Right at this moment I don't think you're popular with anyone. But it could get a lot worse. Dobbin might be prepared to go on giving you rope, but we're not."

"What are you saying?"

"I'm saying you're not the only one who can play tricks. We can too. We can play a trick that will put an end to your jockey hopes forever." The words came out simply, without venom. They didn't frighten Billy, merely made her feel angry at herself again. She wanted to say a heartfelt *I'm sorry*, but the words wouldn't come. By the time they did reach her lips Phil was gone.

*

As Worcester grew nearer things didn't run as planned for Harrup. For a start there was the major obstacle of not being able to contact Jerry Hastings, a popular track bookie and old acquaintance of Harrup's. Finally, fortunately, just a day before the race, contact was made. Hastings hurried up to Rectory and they discussed a variety of matters – working round to Harrup's half-hatched plan. After an hour and a bottle of vodka they were down to the nitty-gritty.

"As far as your book is concerned then, Eeney will be favourite?" Harrup asked.

Jerry Hastings ran a finger round the collar of his dirty white shirt like a character in a gangster movie. He looked a bit like a gangster, with his sleek hair and permanent frozen grin. "As far as everyone's book is concerned," he said suspiciously, "Eeney will be tops. We're talkin' 'bout a fast-footed nag here, Jack. Form's been excellent, with the exception of Sandown. But every geezer's entitled to his off day."

"Well, bear in mind I'm speaking confidentially – " Harrup splashed out more neat vodka from a new bottle.

"You said that three times already, chum. C'mon, you know your old mate. What's the rub?"

"No rub, Jerry. Simply Eeney won't win."

Hastings's eyes sparkled like gems. He eased back the vodka gratefully. "No chance of it?"

"I wouldn't be wasting your time here today if there was."

"All right, if you're certain, Jack. It has to be a no-hoper or I fall a long way, I lose a lot." He appeared uneasy. "Cor, hard to believe that Eeney's in the no-hoper league. You *sure* this is no chancy number? We've had words before about 'maybes'. You know my position with that kind of game – "

"Believe me, Jerry, Eeney will do well to finish the course tomorrow. I don't need to say too much, but I can tell you there's leg trouble. Not obvious, but it's there, and it will stop him."

Hastings considered the kind of money he might make on a

good gate, with heavy takings on the favourite. The stiff smile warmed up. "OK, pal, I guess we can do business on this one. I'll put you in for half. Now, I know we know the rules, but let's run over it again. Eeney will be chalked in at about 6 to 4 –"

The door banged behind them and John Harrup padded in. He had been drinking in Lambourn and had that stupid haughty gaze on his face that his father so disliked. A couple of crumpled newspapers and a copy of *Sporting Life* were wedged under his arm. Without saying anything to Hastings he fell into a fireside chair, kicked off his shoes and began spreading a paper.

Hastings looked warily to Harrup, then across to his son. He reckoned it unsafe to resume the conversation. "Make some tea," Harrup ordered his son.

"Who wants tea? It's only gone lunch, and I can see you two have been keeping your tongues lubricated." John burped rudely. "Anyways, don't want to upset the system." He slapped his stomach. "I always stick to my proper diet, beverages and all, before a race."

Hastings glanced back to Harrup. "Your boy's riding Eeney?"

John Harrup interjected: "I've been riding so well in training, you see. Ol' Dad's been promising me a decent race for ages, so I thought it best to put the gun to his head now."

"You, er, know Eeney?" Hastings pursued.

"One horse's the same as another, surely," John replied stoutly. "I *know* how to race, that's the main thing. Don't worry, Mr Hastings, you keep your odds down. I'll bring Eeney in right up front."

Harrup made a dumb signal to Hastings but the bookie seemed alarmed. Harrup leant forward to whisper, "Don't mind the boy. He doesn't know left from right. Makes no difference what he says. Eeney can't win."

John began prattling on about his diet and his hopes but Hastings stood and gathered his overcoat. Ignoring John he said, "Well, I'm taking your word on this one, Jack. Want to shake on it?"

The two men shook hands and, after the usual pleasantries, Hastings departed. John had seen nothing suspicious. He'd found some sweets in his pocket and was guzzling these as he flicked through *Sporting Life*. Harrup busied himself. He telephoned a large local stables and arranged a place for Eeney in the transporter bound for Worcester tomorrow. Then he sat down to do some accounting sums. After ten minutes the monotonous lazy noises of his son's presence got the better of him. As John popped another toffee into his mouth Harrup exploded: "Why can't you be like everyone else and get on with your work! This is a business we're trying to run here, and you're supposed to be part of it."

"I do my bit!" John shouted. "What d'you think I'll be doing tomorrow – star-gazing?"

"We'd probably all be better off if you were!" Harrup was up and pacing like a caged cat. "You're riding tomorrow for no other reason than that you're the guv'nor's son, let's face it. You're not in trim, you haven't kept any kind of regular training schedule going – "

John laughed aloud. "Neither have you, pops."

Enraged, Harrup's control went. He struck out and hit John across the face. John's head twisted, but he composed himself very fast. When he looked back at his father his eyes were steely and savage. "If I'd known that is what you'd turn out like at seventeen I'd have chucked you into the care of your aunts years ago."

"Oh why don't you shove it." John was staring defiantly at his father.

In order to calm himself Harrup left the house and walked into the brisk chill of the yard. Immediately Pat Devlin intercepted him. "I'm sorry if this is an awkward time, guv'nor, but I must have a word with you."

"About – ?"

"The, er, role of jockey for Worcester." Pat fell into step

beside Harrup. "Y'see, the lads have come to me and put their case. They feel a bit hard done by. By their reckoning Pete or Phil were due to ride tomorrow. They say you promised. They feel John – "

Harrup stopped. "They don't like John?"

"Well, it's not . . . *only* that. I think they all see it as part of their duty to do the best they can by Eeney. Their interest and attention to the horse in the last few days has been great, all of 'em. Pete's a bit lukewarm, but then you know Pete, always is. But Phil has a lot of confidence just now. He thinks he's riding well and feels Eeney's improved a lot. Add that to the fact that, like you say, they feel John's . . . well, they feel he gets it a bit too easy." Pat was prepared for argument, but he had promised the lads he would make their grievance known.

"So, my employees are rising up in arms now, is that it?" Harrup's voice was almost a whisper. As Pat stood still Harrup paced around him for a minute or two, deep in thought. Then he clapped his hands. "Right then, seems like I'd better make a thing or two clear to 'em. Where are they all?"

Pat became flustered. "In the big stable. I have them doing a general sweep up. But – "

"Ideal. Let's be on with it, then." Harrup marched forward while Pat trailed like a wounded dog. What had he got himself in for? Worse: what had he got the lads in for? Maybe he would have been better off keeping his big mouth shut, letting Worcester pass without a row.

Tiny and Billy were on their knees gathering soiled straw and Pete was helping Phil with the sweeping in the stable. They all faltered as the guv'nor came in, tight-lipped and frowning. Pat shuffled after him and shut the door. Billy cringed, expecting trouble.

"All right, you lot," Harrup began. "I'm glad I've got you together. We've rather lost touch with each other over the last few days, but this is entirely my fault. I've been running

71

around the countryside on various, er, errands. Trying to get a bit of important business sorted out. Now – " He eyed Pat coolly. "I've been hearing tales of unrest here, about Worcester. Well, it's understandable I suppose. Nothing official has been made known to you. So, now I'll square the books."

Pete and Phil exchanged a nervous look. They steeled themselves for trouble. Phil dropped his sweeping brush, but grabbed it again in a hurry.

In a business-like dash Harrup resumed: "Eeney has been declared for Worcester tomorrow, so Tiny, you've got to be through with your other horses and had a breakfast by half-nine. You'll be in charge of preparing Eeney. The transporter will be calling at a quarter-to-ten."

"Yessir," Tiny almost clicked his heels and saluted.

"Pete, I know you've been deeply involved with a couple of problems among your charges. I hear tell Domino's got a cold on 'er and Aura Lights has a strain. So, if it's not too much of a disappointment to you, I'd like you to hang about here, take charge while Pat's absent."

Pete nodded, quite pleased apparently.

"And now Phil." Harrup relished the wheezy words. "Seems you've got a lot on your plate with your own team too. But . . . you'll have to get your finger out and have your work done by half-eleven. That's when I'll be leaving here, and I don't intend going without my jockey."

No one spoke. Pat rubbed his ear, making sure his hearing was right. Finally Harrup expanded: "As you'd heard, John was scheduled to ride but, all things considered, I don't think he's fit for it." Under his breath he said, "I bent over backwards to give him his chance." He turned to Phil. "Anyhow, you've been eager to get yourself on, Phil, and I think you're ready for a good race. For a number of reasons I think it's best that we continue to keep Eeney's leg injury to ourselves. I've seen how I can trust y'all. You've done me proud. But the cover-up must go on. There's no shady business, nothing like that. But . . ." Harrup hadn't prepared his lie, but the words rolled out convincingly: "I'm not in the owner's good books and I can't let him know."

A rumble of agreement ran through the group facing Harrup. Everyone seemed happy, but Billy's name hadn't even been mentioned. She was hurt. Through her embarrassment she said, "D'you think I could go along with Tiny tomorrow? I . . ." She lowered her head to hide her blushes. "I feel I might learn something from him about preparing a horse. Then I'll know what to do when my turn comes." She rushed to alter that: "*If* my turn comes."

Harrup's humour was softening. "Very well, my girl. I don't see what harm can be done. Once it's OK by Tiny?"

Tiny, like the others, was only beginning to make his peace with Billy. But he nodded smartly. "Fine by me."

"You've got to do your other work first, mind," Harrup pointed out. "Just because there's an event on doesn't mean a training stables closes down for the day. You'll have to be up no later than *five-thirty*."

Billy blurted, "It's hard enough getting up at six-thirty." The seriousness of Pat's face cautioned her. "But I'll manage somehow. I want to see this race, I want to be part of it."

Harrup gave a short grunt. "Just keep away from Vic Favell. He'll be there and very involved. And for once behave yourself."

Billy smiled gratefully and Harrup walked away as the lads crashed into happy discussion. Pat followed his boss down the stalls, much relieved. Together they entered Eeney's enclosure. "That little talk will do a lot for morale," Pat explained. "The races are the big testers and that's what the lads like to feel they're working for. They want to be part of the action, naturally."

Harrup nodded and cast an eye over Eeney. "Being so busy these last couple of days I haven't had a chance to look at this chappie. How has the rest done 'im?" The answer to that question was there for the eye to see. Eeney looked fresh

73

and frisky, ready for anything. The bandage was off the leg and there was little heat left.

"Remarkable really," Pat enthused. "The rest worked wonders. Like you instructed, we didn't exercise him. But the leg looked so good I couldn't resist taking him out yesterday and today. I was staggered, the improvement has been fantastic."

A frown of real worry etched itself on Harrup's forehead. "I told you to let him rest up, Pat. I didn't want him tested."

"Sure – but you stressed the importance of success at Worcester. When I spoke to you a few days ago you insisted you were going to run him anyway, regardless of the leg, because it left you in with *some chance*. It was *that* desperate." Pat was a bit confused by Harrup's angry expression. "I assumed you wanted me to use my own cop and adjust to the changing situation. You weren't around, Eeney looked better, so I thought – "

"You shouldn't have taken him out." Harrup made no effort to conceal his worry, so great was his shock. Eeney looked *too* good by far.

Pat didn't challenge his boss for a few minutes. Then something jumped to mind, something Harrup had said days ago. Trying to appear nonchalant he asked, "You mentioned some 'emergency plan' for Eeney – would you like to tell me something about it?"

"Plan? What plan?" Harrup was dismissive. He had been a fool to shoot off his mouth so carelessly. Pat was a man of high principles, he would not be the kind to do a deal with the likes of Jerry Hastings. And Harrup must be wary. Many a trainer's reputation – and business – was destroyed by his dabbling in "fixed" races. It was one thing to run a horse with a bad leg and not advertise its past medical history. It was another thing altogether to *guarantee* a bookie that a likely favourite would not be placed. It was the difference between legitimate tactics and out-and-out deception.

Harrup was hemmed in. He had committed himself to

Hastings – and to Phil. But now Phil was on form and the gelding was looking promising. Suddenly the *certainty* was gone. As if voicing his fears Pat said, "We needn't be absolutely pessimistic, y'know. Eeney *could* win."

Una stepped into the stall at that moment. "Mr Harrup. Vic Favell's on the phone. He wants to know the arrangements for tomorrow and he wants you to explain the situation. I tried to sort him out, but he said he wants the facts from your mouth."

# SIX

For Billy the atmosphere at Worcester racecourse was magical. By a coincidence it was at Worcester, as a young child, that she had first experienced the thrill of watching live racing. It had been holiday time, she recalled, and Dad had taken the family for a two-day excursion to nearby Birmingham where Aunt Mim lived. On the second afternoon, with the elder kids in tow, he made for the races. Billy still remembered her initial indifference, then the excitement that hit her like a huge tidal wave. Everything combined to make that day special in her memory and significant in her life: the beautifully groomed animals, the dazzle of jockeys' colours, the eager crowds, the sense of competition and risk.

Now, returning after all these years, Billy was not a wide-eyed child on the sidelines, but a true part of it all. A trainer's lad. As soon as she stepped down from the transporter and smelled the air she was dizzy with pleasure.

It was early, but the bustle was well under way. The first programme was off and the punters were cheering. Loudspeakers carried panting news of the progress of the race. Here, behind the scenes, transporters were arriving from distant stables, racecourse officials were swaggering about, groups of lads were jealously comparing notes.

Tiny was uptight. He had hardly spoken on the long journey down. The transporter had arrived late and he had had time to grow edgy and bad-humoured. Eeney, his pride and joy, had become a little unsettled too. Now he ordered

Billy, "Come on, don't just stand there like a skint punter. Help me get Eeney over to a stall. We're running behind. I want 'im to calm down before he's rushed out to the paddock."

Billy pulled herself together and set to her job. They led Eeney across to a free stall, stripped off his travel rug and gave him a hurried brush down. All the time Tiny whispered away to the gelding, a gentle, calming banter. Billy followed suit and chipped in. Bit by bit they could feel the big horse relax. After twenty minutes they were ready to plait the mane and throw on the elaborate silk-edged show rug. Pat Devlin peeped over the door.

"Running late, Tiny? The guv'nor will be here in the next couple of minutes. And Vic Favell. I want Favell to see Eeney dressed and groomed in the paddock."

"Workin' fast as we can, Pat," Tiny snapped. "Just don't want to upset Eeney, that's the main thing." He turned to Billy and rapped, "Get the good rug shook out. No creases, I want it lookin' like it's never looked." Eeney seemed to give an appreciative sigh and Pat smiled.

"I'll see you at the paddock, Tiny." He raised a hand and made an optimistic fingers-crossed gesture.

Minutes later Phil arrived, white as a sheet. He'd had no breakfast, Billy knew, but he was making a brave show of hiding his nerves. "Learning a thing or two?" he said brusquely to Billy, then stooped to check his ride over. "He's in great shape, Tiny. The leg seems miraculously better. I drove down with the boss. Don't know what he's so glum about. I told him we're in with a great chance but all he kept saying was, 'Don't push Eeney, take it easy'."

"Where's Dobbin now?"

"Favell's just arrived. The guv'nor snatched him up to the bar, I think." Phil gave a little shiver. "Not sure I did the best thing mouthing off like that against John. Suddenly I'm wishing someone else had the saddle today. Pete, anyone!" He glanced at his watch. "Well – must face the music. I'd best take my medical book and go over to meet the valet."

"Good luck," Billy grinned.

"I'll second that," Tiny added.

"Save it for the saddling enclosure, will you?"

When Phil had gone Tiny finished the plaiting, working with loving dexterity. "Bet you'd like to swap places with Phil?" he asked Billy.

Billy surprised herself. "Not really. This is more than just a ride, isn't it? It's not just winning or losing. It's something more and I guess I'm . . . not quite ready for it. Not yet anyway."

"Wise you." Tiny gave her a knowing nod. "This is it, this is what the world of racing's all about. It's big business out there today. Money's going to be won and lost on every single horse running. People are going to walk away rich, and people are going to suffer. It's no different for Dobbin. Rectory is under the microscope here." Tiny rubbed his nose in his pullover sleeve and tied the last knot. "I pride myself on my nose for trouble. I reckon the result of this race'll either perk up ol' Rectory or . . ." he shrugged . . . "maybe destroy it. Lord knows, we both might be out of a job if this swings bad for us. I have this gut feeling."

Someone whistled shrilly just outside and the pair turned to see a young apprentice from Shentons' looking in. They recognised him immediately. It was Jeremy, the boy who had ridden against Phil in the work-out. Then, by a stroke of brilliance, Phil had won by lengths. "Hey, is it true Phil's on Eeney in the 2.15?" he asked. Tiny said yes. "Well, vengeance is sweet, eh! I've been hearing whispers in the bushes, mate. I wouldn't stick a 10p on that old nag today. Looks like I'll have my chance to put Phil in his place sooner than I thought."

Tiny rose aggressively. "You wouldn't chance a penny on Eeney? Worse fool you, chum. I'll lay a fiver he leaves Falcon Tony chewing the hurdles."

"I'll meet that." Jeremy was fully sure of himself. He

looked to Billy. "What about you, girl? Another fiver? I'm open to offers."

Billy wasn't sure of anything any more. She felt cold and tense and the dizzy pleasure she'd felt on arrival had been replaced by a stomach-churning eagerness to get out and *get on* with things. With Tiny's help she smoothed the golden rug across Eeney's back.

"I don't bet," she said. She stood back to play the spectator again as Tiny took the bridle and guided Eeney towards the paddock.

\*

"I'm still none the wiser," Vic Favell said irritably. Harrup just sighed. They were sitting in his Landrover, parked in clear view of the paddock. From the distance they watched the horses. "All you keep saying is my money is assured," Favell went on. "Is this the purpose of engaging an inexperienced apprentice to ride Eeney – so that a lost race is guaranteed?"

Harrup took exception to the slight on Phil's talents. "No, I told you. That must be part of the cover-up. If I employed a more experienced jockey he might detect the bad leg. *Might*, I said. Experienced jockeys and good ones aren't necessarily the same thing." He added sourly, "I always employ good men, Mr Favell. I'm not altogether sure I wouldn't ride Phil anyway if I was looking for the King's Trophy."

"But the boy is going to ride to lose?"

"Look, I'll explain from the beginning: it all depends on creating the illusion that everything is OK. Eeney is entered, fit and liable to win. The jockey lad need know no more than that the leg isn't too good. And he works for me so he's not going to start yellin' out about that. Now, Eeney's form we all know has been good – so the bookies will start him at 6 to 4 or something. Like the rest, my friend Hastings I've been telling you about, will begin offering 6 to 4. Punters will stand off a bit, because the odds are not that encouraging for them. And it's then that Jerry Hastings will *start* – maybe they'll think he's doing it because he's bored, or he's had a look at the horse and doesn't like what he sees."

"Start what?" Favell showed no interest in the horses being paraded in the paddock before him. He was scrutinising his trainer's face.

"He'll lengthen the odds. The others will be offering 6 to 4 and suddenly he'll be giving 13 to 8. So the punters get interested, and the money all goes to Hastings. He's happy to take the flood – but don't forget, he knows Eeney won't win. So the money he's taking is pure profit."

At last Favell was beginning to understand. A wintry grin spread across his craggy face. "I see."

"That's just the start of it. He goes from 13 to 8 on to 7 to 4. More money. Then to 15 to 8. More money. He ends up at 2 to 1 and the punters are queueing to fling down their bets – "

"Fantastic!"

"But that's not the best of it." Harrup had warmed to his own story now and his eyes were aglow. "It's not only the punters who'll fill the kitty. Some of the large betting chains have agents at the track. Now, say one of the big firms has taken three thousand pounds on Eeney at 6 to 4 and their agent sees this joker Hastings offering 2 to 1. What happens? The agent tips off Head Office and they say, *hoi, we'll make a few bob here.* They tell him to put, say, two grand on with Hastings, all quiet like."

"Why?"

"Well, they win every way, don't they? The first thing is they expect the two grand bet to bring the odds down. Say they come down to even money, and Eeney wins. They've got their bet on at 2 to 1, so they get their stake back plus four grand! But they only have to pay back to their punters the three grand they've taken, since the closing price was even money. So, in a sly bit of manoeuvring, they've made a thousand clear profit."

"What if the horse loses?"

"Makes no difference to them, does it? They're betting with the *punters' cash*. If the horse loses, the punters won't be getting anything back anyway."

"It's . . ." Favell the businessman appreciated the irony of the deal . . . "foolproof," he grunted. "Everyone wins except the man in the betting shop." He suddenly slapped Harrup on the back. "Splendid, Jack, splendid. Hastings makes his fortune and you and I get our cut! What could be simpler!" He gave a mocking laugh. "I can't understand why you were so sheepish about it."

Harrup said nothing. He hadn't been bragging because yesterday, like this morning, he had been engulfed in doubts. Inwardly he cursed himself. If he was half a man he'd go to Phil and square up. Lay the law down. Just say, *listen lad, you've got to lose*. But he couldn't. Favell he could trust, because Favell was in desperate straits too. But he could not risk his name with his own employees.

They got out of the Landrover as the horses were led off to the saddling area. Pat Devlin joined them for a chat, then sauntered off. The betting was going precisely as predicted. 6 to 4 as standard, with Hastings beginning to stretch. Favell turned down Harrup's invitation to join him for the saddling. He said he wanted to catch another drink then take up position near the finishing post. Alone, Harrup departed for the saddling area. *En route* he stopped off to observe Hastings's team in action. Hastings and his two clerks were working like Trojans. The queues were starting to form. As Harrup watched, the odds were lengthened again, and more punters flocked up to the box. At the edge of the stands nearby a swarthy young man with a peaked cap was carefully listening to all Hastings's calls. Harrup knew him as an agent for one of the large countrywide betting chains, and guessed it wouldn't be long before, as planned, he'd be running off to telephone his superiors and beg permission for a hefty bet.

In the saddling enclosure Tiny was absorbed in the heavy work. Phil, resplendent in green and gold with a white cap, stood nervously by. Tiny tightened the girth and checked its grip by sliding two fingers under it. "That's the job," he snapped. "Ready for you, Phil."

Phil greeted Harrup dully. "You look spiffing, lad. All set?" Harrup tried to appear calm but noticed Phil's tension. "C'mon now, this isn't your first race."

"Most important yet though," Phil grimaced. "Plenty of encouragement in the air anyway, guv'nor. The betting's good. I feel Eeney has a real chance to – "

"Betting's all right, but it's falling off, Phil," Harrup warned. "Don't get over-eager. One . . . or two bookies are lengthening the odds." He pretended disappointment. "Obviously they've observed Eeney's bad leg. These things are always picked up by the shrewd guys, mark me. Now – I want you to ride well, but extra-cautiously. I don't want bravado. Eeney's a valuable horse. I know what Pat will have said t'you about the importance of a win, but I'd rather end up with a live, healthy animal. Push 'im too far and, who knows, at the end of the race we might be talking about putting him down. Can't have that."

Phil was deflated. "No, sir." With Tiny's help he climbed into the saddle.

"That's the spirit. We know where we stand. Any sign of lameness, pull 'im up. Any doubts – "

Phil brightened. Eeney felt good under him, rippling with energy and ready to go. Without thinking he cut in: "He won't go lame, guv'nor. I feel in my blood he's gonna win."

"Hmm. Very good." Harrup tapped Eeney's flank and turned his face away. "So where's Billy? Up to no good – ?"

"She's been a great help," Tiny said. "Helped cool Eeney after the rush here. I told 'er to grab a sandwich and go to the rails. She'll keep well away from Mr Favell. She's got all the gear ready for the finish – sweat rug, brushes, the lot."

"Excellent. Then all that remains is to say – good luck!" Harrup rubbed his hand down the side of his trouser leg to dry the sweat, then shook Phil's hand.

When he moved off Tiny brought Eeney back out to the paddock while Phil settled in the saddle. Everyone was infected with excitement now. All around the paddock people chewed fingernails and clawed at newspapers. The other mounted jockeys kept their heads down. After a little while a loudspeaker announcement broke the groups up. An official appeared and pointed the first horse towards the starting area. Tiny wished Phil the best, then turned and ran as fast as he could back towards the prime viewing spot at the rails.

He found Billy standing on a crate and elbowed up beside her. They shared a pair of binoculars. "There's Pat having a last word with Phil," Billy told him. "And over there you can see Dobbin with Favell. Look how edgy Dobbin is."

Tiny levelled the glasses and watched. Billy handed him the heel of her sandwich and he chomped it hurriedly. "Eeney's looking good. Calm as a tortoise but nippy on his feet."

"But the betting's shaky. I heard a man a minute ago say some bookie was giving 2 to 1 and it might get longer. Falcon Tony is favourite now. Do you think they realise the problem?"

"Dunno. All I know is I've got a quid on Falcon Tony myself. But, for heaven's sake, don't tell anyone."

Billy gave a guilty chuckle. "You little cheat. Changing spots now, are you? Well, can't say I blame you. This race is anybody's, far as I can see."

Everything happened very fast then. All of a sudden the ten horses were brought into line, a hush had fallen over the crowd and the loudspeaker commentary rasped to silence. Someone beside Billy murmured, "Three miles four furlongs. Quite a run. The horse that wins is goin' to have to have plenty of stamina!"

Suddenly there was an explosion of sound. The loudspeakers screamed, *"That's it: they're off!"* and a powerful cheer soared. Billy grabbed the binoculars and focused on the leading pack. Eeney was well back, but comfortably placed without obstruction. Tiny couldn't see. "How's he going? How's he going?" he shouted into Billy's ear.

"On the inside, nicely placed. He'll have a very clear run into the first fence."

There were three leaders clumped together, then a break of two lengths, then the larger pack with Eeney on the inside. The pace seemed almost leisurely, but every jockey understands that the spectator's view is often misleading. Tiny and Billy knew that Eeney and the others were running hard.

The first fence came and went. One of the leaders stumbled and fell back. Eeney gave no sign of worry or trouble. He cleared well and ran towards the second with enthusiasm. Tiny tried to steal the binoculars from Billy but she stood firm, mesmerised, as for the next half-dozen fences Eeney galloped and glided, showing incredible drive.

By the time Tiny finally got the glasses the leading team was tackling the ninth fence. The field was well divided now. The initial leaders were all gone, trailing far behind. Again and again the thundering voice from the loudspeakers shouted four names: The Seller, Falcon Tony, Rio and . . . Eeney. These four held the front, spread out in a straggly line, but all within fair reach of each other. The rest of the field were suddenly no-hopers.

With half the course to go, Eeney was doing remarkably well. The ninth, tenth and eleventh fences were crossed without incident. The Seller blocked Rio going into the twelfth and both lost a lot of ground. Falcon Tony broke away, two lengths ahead of Eeney, with Rio making up fast.

"Well," the on-course commentator shouted, "it's a three-horse race now. Rio is gaining and Eeney shows no signs of tiring. Falcon Tony is holding on, but . . ." There was the gasping pause as the thirteenth fence was taken. "No, no. That won't do. Falcon Tony's miscued. That's bad. That's opened the door. Eeney is stepping in. Yes, *Eeney is taking the lead!*"

Tiny nearly let the glasses fall. The crowds around him were jostling for position. People hollered, "Come on, boy! Come on, Eeney!" And it was true, Eeney had found a new lease of life. Going like a rocket, he had three lengths on Falcon Tony and Rio neck-and-neck. The leg was holding up superbly and Phil hadn't even taken the whip to him.

The fourteenth was the third fence from home and the excitement on the stands and by the rails had risen to fever pitch. Whichever way, it was clear that it was going to be a close-run finish. The babble from the loudspeakers was inaudible behind the cheering. Tiny could no longer bear to watch. He knew both Rio and Falcon Tony were good finishers. Provided they made the last fences sweetly they would certainly give Eeney a run for his money on the final straight.

From his high vantage point near the finishing line Favell was watching the closing stages in disbelief. Beside him Harrup was struck dumb.

"Fall, damn you," Favell was hissing. "*Fall*. What's wrong with the blasted animal? He's churning up the course!" He half-turned to Harrup. "You said it was all under control. You said Eeney was a write-off. You said the leg would give in – "

"Wait, just wait." Harrup could say nothing more. His mouth was dry and he was clasping the rail before him for support. All the time he was praying, praying. And suddenly, as if in answer to his prayers, the field was changing.

By the far rail Billy, who now had the binoculars, let out a cry of dismay. Tiny tensed. The Seller had begun a last wild charge and had overtaken Falcon Tony. Eeney's lead was slipping and Rio was cashing in. The crowd's call for Eeney was all of a sudden replaced by a scream for Rio.

"Will he make it?" Tiny croaked, covering his eyes.

"One fence to go," Billy said. "It's a clutter now. Can't be a length between the lot of 'em. The Seller is moving like lightning and Falcon Tony won't let him go." Her voice dropped to a low urgent call. "Come on, Phil. Come on. Give him a tap o' the whip."

Phil saw he was running out of ground. Rio was at his elbow and, when he twisted slightly in his saddle, he could see the shadows of the other pair rushing up. He flicked the whip and Eeney responded. The final fence loomed. Like clockwork, three horses – Rio, Eeney and Falcon Tony – went over together. A second later The Seller made it. All landed well, and opened up for the final dash.

*Rio, Rio, Rio!* The chant was frantic, the crowd pressing forward. But, through the din, the loudspeakers were blaring: "It could be Eeney . . . it's neck-and-neck . . ."

Tiny grabbed Billy's arm and shouted for the binoculars, but she shook him off. Her eyes were glued to the last few furlongs stretch and the white-painted finishing post. Rio was edging past Eeney and Falcon Tony was following suit. The Seller was finding his second wind, galloping for all he was worth. Phil threw his back into it, but it was too late. Eeney's breath was gone with only yards to go.

Almost as one the crowd held its breath. The race commentator broke through: "Yes, yes, it's a photo-finish. No! Falcon Tony's across first, with Rio and The Seller a head behind . . . and Eeney, after a truly superb run, falling into a disappointing fourth. Well, what a race!"

Billy lowered the binoculars and moaned. "At least you've covered your losses on Eeney. That bet on Falcon Tony'll square you up."

Tiny didn't look pleased. He turned his back on the track in disgust. "To hell with that. That's torn it. Phil'll be kicking himself. Pat will be mad. Vic Favell won't be too happy. Rectory *needed* that winner. That's the word I got from Pat. I think I'll join you in keeping clear of Vic Favell. I reckon the guv'nor – and all of us – are in for a rocky ride from 'im."

Billy did not speak. She was looking through the binoculars again, scanning the far stands. A curious sight had caught her eye. Dobbin was standing with Favell near the post. They were locked in conversation and, even from here, the tone of their talk was clear. Both were gesticulating hugely . . . and smiling like Cheshire cats.

As owner and trainer of a losing horse, they appeared to be extraordinarily triumphant. Billy was amused, and confused. She turned to consult Tiny but he was gone, making his way hurriedly towards the finish. Back to work.

# SEVEN

During the next two weeks a kind of hard-working normality came to Rectory. Tiny's forebodings proved baseless, Vic Favell was nowhere to be seen and Eeney stayed on, getting fitter by the day. Billy and the rest of the lads were very surprised. Pat had sounded alarm bells, but they had come to nothing. When questioned about it, all Pat would do was shrug his shoulders. "I guess Mr Favell must have been pleased enough with Eeney's performance. After all, the race was *almost* won . . ."

This, to Phil, was like an insult. He brooded endlessly. To his mind the race was lost because of his inexperience. Another jockey, he kept saying, could have forced that last surge from the gelding. At the finish Eeney still had wind in him, and the leg was sound.

It was now that a real mood of friendship between Billy and the boys started to blossom. She consoled Phil, fussing like an old mother, reassuring. To Tiny she provided cheerful hard-working company as she learnt the ropes. Only Pete proved difficult. The more she got to know him, the less she understood. That he was gifted with horses and remarkably intelligent was beyond doubt. Every now and then one could enjoy fascinating conversations with him. But he didn't often come out of his shell, and stayed slightly removed from the other lads. But Billy admired his independent spirit and was annoyed to see Harrup and Pat grow impatient with him. John Harrup positively disliked him, but that was understandable. John had no *way* with horses – several clearly disliked *him* – whereas Pete above everyone had the master's touch. It became second nature with Billy to defend Pete's interests whenever John was around.

When, one wet Friday night, John visited Pat's bungalow at dinner-time all full of smart remarks, Billy was quite ready for him. The chat over dinner had been about Worcester and Phil was once again in depressed form. John had come to deliver some training notes from his father. Immediately he homed in on the conversation.

"Great pity you could do no better than fourth, Phil. But I think it proved a thing or two to Dad, so it served its purpose. You weren't ready for the race."

"I agree," Phil said bluntly.

John was taken aback. He had expected red-faced counter-attack. Una and Tiny were in the kitchen doing the washing-up and Pete was absent, gone to prepare some heavy feed for the morning. Pat busied himself reading the training notes. "It's nice to know there's a sense of reality about the place at last," John persisted. "For a while ol' Dad lost his bearings. Thought he'd got a right little group of Lester Piggotts around him. Thought he was some kind of genius selector. I mean, imagine allowing a girl in as lad!" He sneered at Billy. "And that Pete was supposed to be the great golden hope. Some joke. Seems to me the guy's a sissy. He's afraid to race – "

"If you're referring to the last work-out or somethin' you'd better think again," Billy barked. "You're out of touch, John. Hasn't word reached you yet? Pete didn't ride because I tricked him out of it. *I* wanted his race, it's as simple as that." Before John could answer she rushed on: "Anyway, your character judgements don't count for much here. What would you know about Pete, or any of us? You're never around. You don't bother with the hostel. You look after your measly few charges at all sorts of odd hours when no one ever seems to see you." She pretended a well-meaning shrug. "I

89

may be wrong, John. I don't see you about much. I know you no more than you know Pete."

John's eyes narrowed to slits. "Well, Miss World-wise, you might like to know that I've spent my whole life in the racing game. I have been among jockeys since I was knee-high. I've learnt to see the good ones and the bad ones. I understand the people, the horses, the races. I have more experience than *all* of you rolled into one."

"But you weren't permitted to ride Worcester?"

John nearly fell over in fury. "That was a personal difference of opinion between my father and myself that had nothing to do with readiness or ability – "

Just when it seemed a storm of argument was about to burst Pat cut in: "Well, John, Billy – you know what they say, the deeds talk. In a fortnight's time you'll all have the chance to show your talents." He waved the training notes. "Phil, Pete, Tiny and John will all be riding at races on Bank Holiday Monday. Phil and Pete at Newbury. Tiny and John at Worcester. I'll have the final word on what horses are running where in the next day or two."

"I look forward to that," John said tartly and turned for the door. "Seems to me I've got to show certain people a thing or two about how to ride and how to win."

As soon as the door closed Billy jumped on Pat. "What about me, Pat? Do I get a ride? What's there about me? My four-week testing time's just about up. Mr Harrup said – "

Pat held up a hand. "I'm sorry, Billy. There's nothing for you here. And I'm not going to haggle over it tonight. It's between you and the guv'nor really. I'm sure when the time is right – "

"*When* the time is right! I'll be hearing that till I'm fifty! No. He said a month's trial and I've put my back into it for a month, so now he must decide. Tomorrow I'll talk to him. Tiny did his share and duly got *his* apprenticeship. And Tiny says I'm good, everyone does."

Tiny popped his head round the kitchen door. "Someone

mentioned my name?" He was pulling off the apron smock Una had loaned him for the washing-up.

Pat rose to his feet. "Yes. I was just saying it'd be a jolly good idea to rope Tiny out of the kitchen, get my raincoat on and make tracks for *The King's Cup*. What about it? A few jars'd go down a treat. Cheer ol' Phil up. C'mon. Get your coat on and get Pete, wherever he is."

Una swept into the dining-room. "Smashing. A surprise night out. How kind of you, Pat!" Pat stuttered a bit, hemming and hawing as Tiny ran out into the night. "Well," she said, "you hardly intended to make a stag night of it, did you?"

"Er, no. Sure, you ladies can come along too." He corrected quickly: "Once Billy promises to keep her mouth shut about this apprenticeship."

"Promise," Billy agreed.

"Right, Billy, let's go and get changed," Una suggested.

"Changed? Into what?"

"Into something vaguely resembling nice neat clothes, eh? You've got your mucking clothes on. Doesn't make you look exactly feminine."

"I don't want to look feminine."

Una shook her head. "Come to think of it, with the exception of your travelling clothes, I haven't seen you in anything respectable. Certainly not a skirt or dress."

"*Dress!*" Billy giggled. "I haven't got a dress. I've a pair of slacks I don't much like, then my jeans. These. They do me fine – "

Una had made up her own mind. Taking Billy firmly by the wrist she led her towards her own bedroom. "Well, they won't do you fine in my company at *The King's Cup*. You'll try some of my clothes and look a bit human instead . . . instead of stinking like a walking piggery and looking like one!"

Pat and Phil enjoyed a hearty laugh as Billy was dragged away. A few minutes later Tiny returned, looking downcast.

"Pete says thanks, but no thanks. He'd rather skip it tonight."

"Why? Surely getting the feed ready can't have taken him so long – ?"

"It's not that, Pat. He's over with Domino, giving her a bit of a brush down. Says she's still a bit sweaty after that cold she caught." Tiny made a helpless gesture. "You know Pete. He's quite content to put in extra hours looking after Domino and keeping his other charges company."

Phil sighed. "Don't care what you say, it can't be healthy – all that spare time spent chatting up horses. Last Tuesday he didn't get to bed till near two. I heard him come in and asked him what was up. He said he'd just been sitting with Aura Lights who was restless or somethin'."

Pat addressed Tiny. "You tried to persuade him about the pub?"

"Did my best. Told him we could take a quiet out-of-the-way table if he liked. But no go."

Phil stood up. "I'll have a few words with him – "

"No," Pat put in. "No, leave him tonight. Maybe that's what's wrong. We spend so much time trying to badger the poor chap into doing this or that with his own time." He gave a sly grin. "And anyway, who am I to be discouraging dedication? I reckon you pair could adopt a trick or two of Pete's . . ."

Pat went on talking but suddenly became aware that the eyes of the lads were trained past his shoulder. He looked again and noticed their ox-eyed expressions. "What's taken your – ?" Pat turned as he spoke. His mouth fell open. Billy was standing just inside the bedroom door, Una beside her. Una looked her usual pretty self, but Billy was a sight. The blonde hair was parted neatly and combed behind the ears. There might even have been a touch of lipstick there, Pat decided, for the face certainly looked *new*. But that wasn't the best of it. Billy, the hard-necked yard hand, was actually wearing a *skirt* – skirt and a frilly blouse from Una's wardrobe. Her expression, to match the lads', was priceless. Pat bit his lip to stop laughter.

"Coo-ee!' Tiny gasped. "What's that? Is it a bird, is it a plane!"

"Now," Una said proudly, ignoring Tiny, "doesn't she look good?"

"Hey," Tiny came back, "Billy's a *girl*, I think."

"Wow!" Phil was joining the fun; they both stalked round her as though she was some wild creature. "How come we never realised! She *looks* like a girl, she smells like a girl, she talks – "

Billy took her cue. She waved a clenched fist towards Tiny. "One more comment, from either of you, and you get this gift-wrapped. Right?"

"Enough said," Una interjected. She pulled Pat up. "I give in. Before the feathers start flying I suggest we all put up a brolly or two and make for the mini-van."

Outside the rain was falling with the force of a dam-burst. From the corner of one of the open stables Pete watched while the crowd from the bungalow piled into Pat's battered mini-van. For the tiniest fleeting moment he envied them and wished he'd accepted Tiny's invitation. But then he thought again of his horses, his true friends, and his heart settled. He walked back to the big stable and went to Aura Lights' stall.

A couple of weeks ago the horse had rolled over in his stall and crashed a leg against the woodwork. Nothing more than a hot strain resulted, but Aura Lights had been lucky. Horses have been known to break legs in such a roll. By now the leg was repaired but the horse had had little exercise these last weeks and was restive. On Wednesday, without consulting Pat, Pete had taken him out. They'd had a good gallop, which Aura Lights enjoyed. But yesterday and this morning Pat had only allowed a mile-long trot. Pete sensed the horse needed something more taxing.

As he thought about Aura Lights, Pete became aware of a second motor engine firing into life. Just as Pat's mini-van faded away, another vehicle was drawing out. Running to the door, Pete glanced into the yard. Sure enough, Dobbin's Landrover was moving off. The short figure of the guv'nor, trilby tilted down on his forehead, could be clearly seen behind the wheel. In a minute the yard was silent again. Pete took stock. The coast was as clear as could be, and Aura Lights could be tacked up and ready to ride in five minutes!

Working at speed, Pete prepared the horse, then threw on an oilskin wrap and old woollen cap. He led the horse out, closed the stable, then mounted. It was obviously unsafe to wander far, so he made for the manege. Once there, Aura Lights perked up and became his old responsive self. "Good fella," Pete purred. "Let's have a hundred circuits and a bit of cross-jumping, OK?"

The horse cantered happily, head boldly up to the rain. Pete was delighted. The rain meant nothing to him. All his attention was fixed on the horse's gait and rhythm. "That's a fella. Up, now. A bit faster. Head up." He spoke briskly but with affection, and the horse trusted him fully and charged on in the darkness.

"*What d'you think you're up to!?*"

Icy waves washed down Pete's spine and he almost toppled Aura Lights. Automatically he pulled up, tearing hard on the reins. He swivelled, searching the darkness for the source of the voice. Who was it? Who had spoken?

"I said, what are you at? Playing Indians or something, at this hour of the night?"

Pete's eyes adjusted to the blackness that surrounded the manege and he picked out the slim figure approaching. A second later he saw it was John Harrup. *John.* Why hadn't he remembered John? Only very infrequently did John ever go with the others to Lambourn.

"I'm, er, I'm just giving Aura Lights a small run. I thought he needed something to quieten – "

John came to the fence and tugged the horse's bridle. His face was angry, "*You* thought! You know what would happen

94

if my father saw you, don't you? You'd be packing your cases and getting the next train."

Pete immediately dismounted. There was little point in apologising to John, but he knew he was in the wrong. "I don't make a habit of this, and I won't do it again," he said. "But there won't have been any damage done. Aura Lights likes soft ground and the bad leg is healed."

"That wouldn't cut any ice with my father, I'd guess. Nobody has the right to re-jig training schedules except Pat Devlin, and then only in special circumstances. Riding out after dark like this is sheer madness."

"I told you it won't happen again."

John wasn't yet satisfied. There was still fun to be had from this squirming fish at the end of his line. "They say you're horse-crazy, Pete? I've even heard Una say you're only short of moving your bunk into the stable."

"You know my fondness for horses. I've worked with 'em one way or the other for near ten years."

"Then it's gonna' be a shame to have to give it all up. What with jobs being so hard to come by – "

"I'm askin' you, John. Please, let this drop. I shouldn't have ridden Aura Lights out and I'm sorry. I'd appreciate if you'd say nothing to your Dad."

"That might be . . . arranged."

There was silence but for the drumbeat of rain. "I'm listening."

"Good." John was still holding on to the horse while Pete stood, arms limp. "The older I get the more I'm thinkin' I'm, well, taken for granted around here. People don't seem to realise I've been in the saddle since I was four, that my experience far surpasses anyone else's. *I* am the ace jockey here."

"You've had plenty of important rides in the past few months."

"That's not the point. I'm treated like muck. For example, it seems to me I'm overloaded with unnecessary stable work.

Feeding, mucking, polishing saddles – you know what I mean."

"I think I get the point."

John's eyes were suddenly diamond lights in the murk. "I'm glad you do. I'm glad you're so devoted to horses as well. You'll obviously be very pleased to start looking after some of *my* chores." When Pete didn't instantly reply John goaded, "You do want to stay on here I presume?"

"Yes. I want to stay on."

"Then I think we have a deal, Pete." John's teeth sparkled in a grin. He handed the reins of Aura Lights back to Pete and bade him goodnight.

*

Harrup put down the bedside phone. He had just been speaking to Vic Favell. He lay back in the pillows and gazed towards the streaming morning light. So Favell was happy, but screaming for his money. Harrup had explained that there'd been a minor delay with Jerry Hastings, but all would be resolved within forty-eight hours. In fact, later today he would be meeting Hastings in Lambourn and hoped to have the cash then.

"I still haven't quite got over the shock of that race," Favell had said brightly. "Up to the final straight the beast had me fooled, I thought he'd won."

"I've always said Eeney was a fine horse." Harrup had taken the opportunity to remind the owner. "Of course *I* knew the small leg strain would stop him. But it was only a trifle, y'know. Our stables take excellent care of the horses, Mr Favell, always have."

There had been a dry cough down the line, as though Favell was steeling himself to say something naughty. "Well, I can only say I'm very satisfied. Perhaps, er, we can try this trick again. You'll be entering Eeney for Worcester again in a fortnight?"

Without thinking Harrup had replied; "He'll be entered

all right. But, like I said, he's a great horse and he's on the mend. You can put money on him this time. Money to win. Big as you like – because I can assure you he's going to mop up that course . . ."

After Harrup rang off that snatch of conversation ran and re-ran through his head. It was easy to see why Favell wanted another deal with Hastings. Without risking a penny of his own cash he had made a fine profit. Something over fifteen hundred, Harrup guessed. Maybe more. But, by comparison, Harrup wouldn't do so good. The "fix" had certainly got him out of a hole with Favell – but the overriding problem of making ends meet at Rectory remained. A hundred and fifty quid wouldn't go very far towards paying overdue feed bills and the various hire purchase instalments.

No, Harrup had been forced to think about new ways of getting some money for himself. Worcester had been a shocker all right, but it showed what the horse *could* do. Maybe with another, better jockey, with ample training . . . Without actually sitting down to reason it all out, Harrup had more or less decided that Eeney was salvation. The gelding must be trained hard and made to win. *Fast*. Harrup could then beg, borrow or steal some good cash and slap it on Eeney's nose. That way he could capture really substantial returns . . .

Suddenly, after the phone talk with Favell, that plan didn't seem so good. Something else found its way into Harrup's brain – a half-formed notion that might, just might, prove easier and more rewarding. Harrup stopped himself from analysing it. Once again the whole idea was based on deception, and he had no intention of burdening himself with guilt for the day.

But, try as he did, the fresh plan rang through his head when he opened his mail and found handfuls of unpaid bills. It rebounded again when the insurance man called, and later some reps. from feed suppliers, all looking for monies due.

Hastings phoned at five, requesting a meeting in the car

park at *The King's Cup*. Harrup drove there in a dream, the plan hammering away at the back of his mind. By the time he'd parked the Landrover beside the bookie's big car he was decided. Plan One was out the door: he wouldn't risk a hefty bet on Eeney's next race. Plan Two would be tried instead.

Hastings greeted him with a nod and a smile. Immediately he passed over the fat envelope. "Sorry 'bout the delay," Hastings said. "My finances were up in the air for a couple of days. My accountant's been in doin' the books and I froze everything for a bit."

"That's all right." Harrup burrowed slightly down in the passenger seat of the bookie's car and opened the envelope. A stack of crisp fifty-pound notes winked up at him. "This is half the taking?"

"Yep. Two thousand two hundred and eighty. Not bad for ten minutes' work, eh?"

"Whew! Lot better than even I thought."

"You know me, Jack. Fair dealer. The betting was heavy, I'm glad to hand it over. You get another touch like that, mate, don't forget to throw it my way. Only don't make the nag come so close to winnin', will ya?"

Hastings was already reaching for the ignition, waiting for Harrup to get out of the car. "Just a second, Jerry," Harrup pleaded, pocketing the cash. "Something's been rolling through my mind today. I was wondering . . . well I mean, this business worked so well, why don't we give it another go? The same scheme with the same horse. He's running again at Worcester in a fortnight. I can make certain he doesn't win – "

Hastings sat back, grim-faced. "Um. Dunno, Jack. Eeney won't be favourite next time, so he won't attract the greedy masses going for longer odds."

"Maybe not, but he'll most likely be second favourite. So there'll still be a lot of money on him and if we know he's not going to win, just like last time, it's all profit to us."

"I'm not sure, pal." Hastings lit a cigarette with concentration. "It's all a bit close to the other venture. It might look suspicious."

"Not necessarily. You can play it straight this time. *Don't* lengthen the odds – then nobody can suspect you've got inside information."

Hastings's eyebrows shot up. "But if we don't stretch the odds, Jack, we don't take the money. We get bits of it, fine – but so does every other track bookie."

Harrup slumped back, frowning. "Yes, I see what you mean."

Hastings gave Harrup a friendly nudge. "Look, mate, give it a few months. Come back to me with another worthy nag and we'll talk business again. OK?"

"I'm not sure I'll still be in the training game in a few months, Jerry. That's the trouble."

"Come off it, Jack. That envelope in your pocket's got over two big ones in it – "

"That's my trouble. The money's not mine, it's the owner's. It was one of *those* sort of deals. For the good of my health, but not my pocket – if you get my meaning. My stake's a rotten ten per cent."

"That all!" Hastings recoiled in surprise. "Cor, Jack, doesn't seem to have been really worth your while at that rate. You must certainly have been down on your knees to the owner, eh? I've heard of charity, but that's ridiculous."

Harrup leant forward to drive his point home. "That's exactly it, Jerry. I've had this bloke breathing down my neck, there was nothing I could do. All right, so I've shaken him off with this tidy little bundle and his horse is still respectable. But *I'm* no better off. This morning it hit me like a ton of bricks. This system is foolproof – and now *I* want to benefit from it." He paused and said coldly, "I have to, Jerry. It's no whim. I'm asking you . . . as a favour. I'm a proud man and I don't like making my business known, but I'm in a corner. There's no point in mincing words. The way I reckon, I'll be out of business in a month unless I can get my hands on ready cash. Two or three grand would be ideal just now – "

An impatient, harsh look darkened Hastings's face. He hated sob stories, he'd heard enough to last a lifetime during his years at the track. "All right, suppose we do chip in again – what if Eeney wins?"

"No chance, I'll make sure of it."

"Tell me how, Jack. You said that last time, but the geezer almost came home."

"Yeah, well it won't happen this time. This time I've a different jockey, a whole different approach in mind."

"So you'll cover my losses if he *does* win?"

Harrup blinked his eyes and half-laughed. "There's no point even talking 'bout it. He won't come anywhere near winning." Hastings did not appear convinced. He sat steadily smoking, staring Harrup. "OK, if you want guarantees – I *will* cover you in the event of a win. But – "

"What with, Jack? You say your financial situation is bad." He spread his hands and his voice became soft, reasonable. "I'm in business. I'm sorry, but I allow no margins of error."

"Fine, fine. I understand. I'll cover you . . . with my Landrover. That should more than clear any losses. It's only a few months old, as you can see."

Jerry Hastings looked the Landrover over carefully from the window of his car, then shrugged. "I guess I can't go far wrong. All right, you have a deal. Eeney loses again at Worcester."

*

It had begun to feel a bit like Christmas for Tiny. This was three times in a couple of days he'd been invited into Lambourn for a knees-up. Pat was buying the rounds again this evening. Tiny was on top of the world. He had a lot to celebrate: for a start there was the signing up of the apprenticeship papers last week. Then the news that Harrup had assigned him a ride at Worcester in a fortnight. Everything was suddenly looking very rosy indeed.

They had parked the mini-van in front of the pub because the car park appeared full. Now they marched around the neck of the car park, towards the pub's main side entrance. Tiny was whistling blithely to himself but Pat suddenly pulled up. Tiny stopped. "What's wrong?"

"Nothing. Er, look, I didn't lock up your door of the van. You go on in. I'll be with you in a jiffy."

"Ho, tryin' to skip the honours, eh?"

Pat pressed a fiver into Tiny's hand and gave him a playful push. Tiny disappeared through the side door, laughing.

Pat stood still a moment, then walked a few steps through the maze of parked vans and cars. He drew back in the shadow of a horse-box, waited, then peeped out again. Sure enough, he wasn't wrong. There was Jerry Hastings all right, with Harrup beside him in his car. They were beaming and shaking hands, but there was something odd about them. Maybe it was Harrup's habit of constantly glancing sideways, as though expecting – and dreading – to be seen. Or maybe it was just the very fact of sitting in conversation out here, and not in the warmth of the bar.

Pat frowned. He knew Hastings of old and was wary of him. There was nothing positive to suggest he was a baddie, but Pat had heard a whisper or two . . . He realised he was being nosy – that instinct and prejudice were running away with him. Big deal – so *he* didn't like Jerry Hastings. Too bad. But the guv'nors associations were none of his business. He had a job, Harrup paid his wages – that was all there was to it.

He moved back towards the pub, but the thought wouldn't leave him. Was it possible that the guv'nor and Hastings were on to some kind of fiddle?

# EIGHT

The ground on the gallops was rock hard under frost at eight next morning. Billy was pleased because Misty, her mount, liked the going firm and never shied away from a bit of frost. But Tiny, riding alongside her, was less than enthusiastic. He gripped the reins tight and rode stiff-backed, with great care.

"You're spoiling that horse," Billy complained. "She's not afraid of a hard surface. Come on – race you to the end! Last in does the washin'-up for the rest of the week."

Tiny hadn't the chance to decide either way. Billy reached out and slapped his horse, then jabbed her own. Both leapt away. The pace was good but not frantic. Both rode well, but Tiny's heart just wasn't in it. Billy cleared the course lengths ahead of her rival, then reined in. She twisted in her saddle to watch Tiny's approach, but Tiny pulled in yards short of the finish line.

"What's the matter with you?" Billy shouted. "Getting yellow at the sight of a little ice? It's quite safe. Pat said – "

"To hell with Pat." Tiny moved slowly up, one hand gently massaging his forehead. Billy hadn't really looked him over properly this morning, but now she did she saw he sported the complexion of a marble statue. "You ever tried to gallop with a headache?" he asked. "I feel like someone's whacking the back of my neck with a mallet." He grimaced. "And it's all courtesy of Pat Devlin." Tiny's mind reluctantly jerked back to last night. The first couple of lemonades were all right, but he had ended the evening on a few glasses of rough cider.

Billy wasn't sympathetic. "Serves you right for being silly, then. Never mind. A brisk run will do you all the good in the world. Let's do the full circuit. Remember you've to get in trim for next week."

"Forget it, I can't gallop. Not today."

They were interrupted just then by the sight of another rider, cutting towards their run. "Hey, it's Pete," Billy called. "But what's he doing on Dot? I thought Dot had been passed back to John's care? *He* was exercising her last week."

Pete hadn't seen the others until it was too late. From afar the run had looked deserted. But now here was Tiny and Billy, tucked behind the fence, slap in his track. He slowed the horse and gave a vague wave.

"You looking for extra work?" Billy said. "You've already had Domino out. And you've plenty more to do. What's up?"

"It's OK, just that John's tied up."

"So what? *I* was all tied up myself. In the bedclothes. Since when have we started doing favours for John? Didn't I see you yesterday cleaning some of his tack?" Little flickering memories were coming to Billy – odd incidents observed over the last two days. "What is this with you and John?"

"Don't be crazy. It's nothin'. I'm just riding Dot out because I want to. Right?" Before anyone could answer Pete had spurred his mount away.

Billy sat gazing after him in amazement. "Well! What d'you make of that? Smells fishy to me."

Tiny shuddered in the cold. His head was swimming and the restless movements of the horse under him were beginning to take their toll. "Pete is the best judge of his own affairs," he said. "And I'm just beginning to realise I'm getting seasick out here." He turned his horse for home. "I'm packin' in for the day. Dobbin said he'd be out to see us ride, so if he comes spin him a yarn. I'm gonna take a couple of pills and bury my head in a pillow."

As Tiny trotted off Billy yelled after him, "Goodnight, sweet prince. Remember, you're for the washin'-up for the rest of the week." She sat back in the saddle and mused. No one had told her Harrup was coming on to the gallops this morning, but she was glad he was. For days she had been trying to corner him, to question him about the likelihood of her apprenticeship. But every time she got close there was an excuse – he had a prior engagement, or was tired or had a phone call to make. But today he wouldn't get away . . .

Just at that moment Billy heard the purr of the Land-rover's engine. She decided to act there and then.

Harrup looked like a bull with a sore head. His eyes were red-shot and his skin blotched, as though he'd had a hard night on the beer himself. As Billy cantered up he pointed to the gallops. "What's this supposed to be? Lunch-hour or breakfast? Where is everyone? Don't you all realise we're running a business here? I can see Pete. Where's Phil and Tiny?"

"Tiny had a bad headache, he went back to take some tablets. Phil's finished his first exercise, he's gone for the second – "

"Madness," Harrup grunted. "I'll have to have a word with Pat about arranging proper strings. This random work-out procedure's been taken advantage of while I'm breakin' my back trying to keep a stables going! I'd be better off sellin' out here and now, let you all go to the Job Centre."

Billy hesitated. She had picked a bad time to confront the guv'nor – but then every time seemed to be a bad time with him. She sucked in air and said, "I'd like a word with you here and now. I was wondering whether you'd any news for me yet?"

"News? What about? You've been muttering on about something for days – "

"You know what about. You told me I was on a month's trial. You said you'd review things in a month. The month's up."

Harrup looked fit to explode. "It's been a busy time, you know. I haven't had time to think about small matters. Give me a week or two – "

"Oh, be fair! I've worked hard and I've been patient. I've done my share. You must be able to decide now. Am I to have my apprenticeship?"

"Dammit, girl, we've all worked hard. There's more to consider than that."

"More? Like what?"

"Like whether I'm going to be in business *next week*!" Harrup regretted the words as soon as he'd said them. It was bad enough to have to bare all and crawl for Jerry Hastings's support. But to beg this hungry girl's understanding – that was something else altogether. Angrily he said, "I've warned you before not to nag me. Look, I'll concede that you're a good rider and have every chance of making a good jockey some day. But, for various reasons, I can't give you a yes or no at the moment. Don't think your earnest work has passed unseen. I've heard good reports from Pat and the lads. You're bright, and you're learning. Don't throw all that away." Almost without pausing for breath he rushed on: "Now have I told you about next Monday? Obviously I haven't. You've got an outing and you're in charge. The place is Worcester and the horse is Eeney again. This time you'll take the role Tiny took at the last race. D'you think you can manage that?"

Taken by surprise, Billy could only mumble: " 'Course I can. Eeney and me get on fine. But what about Mr Favell?"

"Forget Favell, I'll look after him. Tiny can't do it anyway, because he'll be racing himself that day. All the lads will be riding."

Billy was reminded of the injustice of it all. "Everyone except me," she said.

"Your turn will come."

"There's lots of horses in the stables fit to race. Why can't I ride? Is it 'cause I'm not an apprentice?"

"No, it's nothing to do with that. You don't have to be an apprentice to ride. All you need is a licence and you've got one."

"Have I?" Billy cheered up.

"Yeah, I take out a licence as a matter of course for all the lads who work for me."

"So, OK, forget my apprenticeship. Why can't I ride on Monday?"

"Because I haven't got a horse for you. You're wrong, girl. There's *no* other horse ready to race at this time. And the other lads come first. Even you must see that."

Billy tried to pursue the matter in vain. Harrup became quite ratty. "I've had enough," he said. "There's Pete and Phil now lining up for a gallop. Take Misty over and join 'em. Let's stop the nonsense and get a bit of work done . . ."

Billy trotted back to the chalked start line biting her lip. That was it, then. The cards were on the table and there was to be no apprenticeship. The best she'd done was a temporary promotion: charge hand for a day with Eeney at Worcester. And that only because no one else was available to fill the gap. Was that progress at all? Or had these last busy weeks at Rectory been a waste of time?

Billy was near despair. She felt even worse because she had grown to care for Rectory, and the lads. She wanted their respect, and she wanted to be one of them. It wasn't merely an apprenticeship she now sought, but a *Rectory* apprenticeship – to learn and grow and challenge with Pete and Phil and Tiny.

*

"Don't take it too bad," Tiny consoled Billy. "Very few people come straight in, do their month and get the apprenticeship. I was here a bit before I went on trial."

"Yes, but he *promised* me. He said he'd consider over the four weeks."

They were toiling side by side in the tack room, washing

and polishing bridles and saddles. Tiny's headache had gone but his work movements were careful and slow. Behind them, at a corner bench, Pete was labouring furiously. Billy hadn't taken much notice of Pete but when she turned and saw what he was doing she was quickly diverted from self-pity. "Here, Pete," she snapped, "what are you doin' with that harness? That's not for you to rebuild! It's Phil's, isn't it? Or John's –?"

Before Pete could reply John Harrup sauntered in, the saddle of one of his charges hooked over his arm. He had been exercising – rather late in the day – but was now changed into casual town clothes. His appearance was in stark contrast to the others. His shoes were sparkling and his fair hair was freshly washed. "So this is where it all happens?" he grinned. "Like working down the mines, I suppose."

"You suppose?" Billy said sarcastically. "Pity you don't *try it* more often. Then you'd *know*. Great education, this is."

John glowered like a vicious animal. Then he calmed down, and threw his saddle on the bench in front of Pete. "There's a good chap, do that one for me while you're at it." Pete said nothing; just pulled the gear towards him. John smiled back to Billy. "I've been meaning to ask you," he said sweetly. "I'm going into Lambourn for a drink. Like to come?"

Tiny nudged Billy hard in the ribs. "Hey, think he fancies you. This is your big chance. Wine and dine with the top nob's son."

Billy laughed. She spoke off the top of her head. "You must be joking! I wouldn't been seen dead with that. What's he dressed up for? A party political broadcast?"

"Just as well." John's expression was deadpan. He plunged his hands into his jacket pockets and tilted his chin up proudly. "My regular place doesn't like customers who stink of horse muck."

Billy grew red. "Why don't you do us a favour and push off – "

"No," John chuckled drily. "Why should I deny myself the pleasure of watching the riff-raff work?"

Billy took the insult personally. Very slowly she paced towards the corner. "You just don't take hints, do you?" She gathered up the saddle John had just put down and, in a sudden jerk, flung it towards him. Winded by the force and weight, John collapsed against the wall. The saddle crumpled on to the ground. "Maybe this'll get the message across. You either work here or you don't. If you don't, then get out. If you do, join the riff-raff. I'll lend you a polishing pad."

Billy went to turn her back on John but suddenly he cried out. "You little devil! Take that up. *Now*. Take my saddle off the floor!"

"Get it yourself."

John reached behind him and pulled a whip from the wall rack. He held it up, ready to strike. Billy stood not five feet away from him. "I won't tell you again. Take up my saddle."

In a fast deft dart, Billy had reached across John and yanked down another horse whip. Like John, she pushed it forward threateningly. "You dare touch me with that and you can bet your life you'll end up crawling out of here."

John grimaced and prepared to lash down.

Billy stood her ground. "Come on, use it. See what you get. Hit me."

The two whips stood poised in mid-air for all of three minutes. John's held high, aimed for Billy's face; Billy's jutting out, half-ready to ward off a blow. Finally John backed down. He threw his whip aside and scrubbed a hand across his face, wiping sweat off. "You're a fool," he said. "I'm going to get you the sack from here."

Billy moved to lunge bitterly but the door beside her banged open. Harrup stepped in, sensing the aggression instantly. "What is going on here? What's the shouting for? You can be heard in the yard."

John nodded towards Billy. "Sack her."

"What! What're you talking about, lad?"

"You heard me – give her the sack. Right this minute."

Everyone froze, but Harrup's response came unexpected. Turning on John, he struck out and slapped him across the face. "You talk to me like that again, sonny, and I'll belt you from here to Christmas. Clear off outa' here!"

Reeling towards the door, John grabbed the handle to straighten himself. He stalled a second, but the tone of his father's voice left no doubt as to his earnestness. Ducking clear of a possible second blow, he vanished. Harrup faced the stunned group. "What was all that about?" He saw the whip dangling from Billy's hand. "No, on second thoughts, don't tell me. I don't want to know." He gave a short plaintive sigh. "All of you – just try to keep out of trouble. Especially you, girl. I'll say it once. I don't ever want to repeat it."

When he was gone Tiny gave Billy a comradely pat on the back. But Billy crossed to Pete. "Why are you doing his work?" she asked him. "It's obvious as anything now, so don't try to hide it." Pete shuffled his feet, embarrassed. "You've been doing his grooming, and when he handed you that saddle you didn't even murmur."

"I'm just helping him out. Don't make a big issue of it."

"Pete – there's got to be another reason. You're an easy-going sort, but even you wouldn't do those kind of favours for John. Has he been threatening you in some way? Because that'd be his style, wouldn't it?"

Pete held out for a few minutes but finally threw the towel in. The truth was there for anyone to see. "It's a bit of a mess," he said at last. "John saw me riding Aura Lights after dark in the rain. The horse was recovering from a strain and I had no one's permission."

"What's so bad about that?"

"You get the sack for that kind of thing, Billy. The danger of cantering round in the dark is clear – for horse *and* rider. This isn't a kiddies' riding school, you know. It's a professional training stables, full of horses worth thousands of pounds . . ."

Billy flopped down on a stool. "So John saw you and put the screws on? Some pal he is, eh? Why couldn't he have just argued the toss with you, left it at that?"

"Like you say, Billy," Tiny cut in, "that's not his style. He has his private way of doing everythin'."

Billy suddenly felt as though she was back in Burnham, playing Mum to the kids. The old protective nerve sprang to life again. Pete was too decent a guy to suffer John's mean cunning. "I think we're going to have to do something to teach John a lesson," she said.

"How?" Tiny was pleased to be involved.

"Don't know," Billy muttered, nibbling her thumb in concentration. "But I'll think of something."

*

Harrup caught up with John walking through the forest that ringed the stables. John was furious after his father's attack, feeling he'd been made a fool of in front of the others. When Harrup approached he made to run, but Harrup caught his arm. "Wait a minute, laddie," he implored. "No need for hysterics. Slow down." John reluctantly stopped, but wouldn't look at his father. Harrup calmed his own breathing and tried to sound reasonable. "Now, what was all that about in there?"

"It's Billy," John stammered out. "She's trouble, a stirrer . . ." His voice cracked with emotion.

"All right, all right. Ease down. If she's a stirrer keep out of her way."

"She's not going to push me around – "

"No one's gonna' push anybody around."

John was suddenly bold. "That's rich coming from you." As he spoke he took a small step back, as if readying himself for further assault.

Harrup shrugged and sat down on the fallen trunk of a

dead oak. His brain was racing. This row, today of all days, was unfortunate. Today he had intended to make his peace with John, to beg a favour. In a cool tone he said, "You deserved that whack I gave you, son. Fair's fair. If I let you talk to me like that in front of the staff everyone would be at it. I'd have no authority left." He waited a minute for that to sink in, keeping his eyes off John and on the blade of grass he was shredding with a thumbnail. He wanted desperately to restore calm, to create an atmosphere of chumminess that was once, long ago, quite easy with the lad. Eventually he looked up again. The burning colour was fading from John's cheeks. "Anyway, the incident's over and done with. In the past we've had our differences. But the past is over and done with, son. You and me have to start getting on. We're going to have to work as a team . . . if we're to survive."

John wasn't impressed by what sounded almost like a threat. "I'm not a child," he said. "We've had our differences all right, and you've made the jockey stakes hard for me at times. You've dropped me from races, claimed I wasn't fit enough, swore I didn't work enough – "

"Maybe." Harrup had to struggle to keep an even tone. "Maybe, but I've also given you the kind of breaks other kids never get. You were running in major races earlier than most. You had a success or two, but lots of failures. I could have listened to those who advised me to chuck you." He saw John was about to flare up and raised his voice: "*But* I kept my faith in you. In time, I reckoned you'd be good. I still do. And I hope I'm proved right. Because, lad, we do need to swing together. Badly."

The intensity of Harrup's expression intrigued John. "What are you saying?"

Harrup was forced into frankness. He said, "The money situation is very bad. Either I get some cash to pay the bills soon, or I face the risk of having to close the place down." Shrewdly he added: "If that happens you're at the mercy of new employers – if you can find 'em."

"It can't be that bad."

"It is."

John was genuinely shocked. His father was a man of few words, and was never a scaremonger. "This situation must have been developing over a period of time," John said. "Why didn't you tell me?"

"The only times I've seen you we've argued. I suppose it's been as much my fault, because the pressure of worry has been getting me down. But the signs were there, John. I'm sure by now quite a few people have begun to nurture doubts about Rectory's future."

John sat opposite his father, winded. He had never contemplated life outside Rectory's protective umbrella. He had never contemplated serious challenge or serious work. He ran a hand through his longish hair and said, "Can anything be done to save things? Is it too late?" There was anxiety in every breath.

Satisfied at last, Harrup leaned forward. "No, we have a hope. *If* we work together."

"I can help – ?"

"Next Monday you're riding Eeney at Worcester. You have to make him lose."

"But I've been out with Eeney over the last few days. He's burstin' to go. He's fit to win, even Pat says so. And if you bet on him, you'll win."

"It's a complicated business and you don't need to know about it, but I can tell you if he loses I'll get more." He paused and stared at his son. "It's already fixed. Everything depends on you now."

John thought for a moment. "From what I've been told the field won't be that great. And the word going round is that Eeney's hot. If I bring him slow it won't do my riding record much good."

"Face it, John. If I have to close down the stables next month it won't do your riding any good at all."

"No, I can see that – "

"So, will you do it? Everything rests in your lap."

"It's no question really, is it?" John stood and ambled in a circle, hands crushed into pockets, kicking the dead winter leaves. "Very well, I agree. I'll do it . . ."

"Good lad."

". . . on condition. On condition that you do something for me in return."

Harrup drew back, puzzled. "Like what?"

"Sack the girl."

Harrup didn't try to hide his annoyance. "Oh, for heaven's sake! C'mon. You had your row, it's over. Just forget it."

John spun on his father, full of the old bitter arrogance. "I don't like her and I don't want her around. Apart from anything else she's not good for this stables. You're asking me to do something for the good of Rectory, so I'm asking you the same. If you want me to make Eency lose, you sack Billy."

All Harrup wanted was a peaceful world, a speedy end to his financial worries. He stood and made a gesture of surrender. "I can't do it till after next Monday because I need a help here. I'm running four horses and hoping to pick up pocket money on the other three – "

"You can sack her the day after the races if you want. That suits me. Just as long as you promise here and now that you're going to do it."

Harrup sighed and linked his son's arm. They turned towards the house as a heavy afternoon drizzle started to fall. "All right, son, it's agreed," Harrup said. "Consider the girl fired."

"Very good. Now let's get down to the nitty-gritty. If Eency must lose I'd like to make it look as convincing as possible. As far as I can, I want to avoid any possible mark against my reputation. Just holding him back can be risky – "

"There's plenty we can do to cover you there. There are a

few days to go till the race. We can show Eeney to be off-form at the gallops, just among our own boys and the locals. I'll show you a few tricks to make him jump wide and generally look bad." Harrup thought for a second, searching for ideas. "I'll have a word with the others. From now on you lad for Eeney. I'll sort that out with Tiny who's been looking after him. Tiny can swap the black filly with you."

"I don't want *more* work, you know – "

"I'll lend you a hand, don't worry. But this can help us . . . *you*. We can play a trick and substitute feeds. Give Eeney some mash every day to fatten him up and make him sluggish. Give 'im more than he needs, pamper him to death – eh? And let him have a bucket of water early on the morning of the race. That's sure to slow him down."

"Yes, yes . . ." John's eyes were shining in delight. "That would take the fizz out of him all right." He laughed, thinking of Pat Devlin and the others, and of all their pathetic hopes for Eeney. "This is beginning to sound like fun," he said.

# NINE

Preparations for the Bank Holiday races threw Rectory into turmoil. For a while it seemed as if Harrup had taken leave of his senses. Schedules were juggled and re-sorted. Charges were swapped around. One day Dot was to be declared for Newbury, with Phil riding; next day it was Just Nicola. For a week Tiny had believed he was to be riding Eeney, then word filtered back that John had the job. Confirmation finally came from Pat, with the news that John was also to lad for Eeney till Monday.

"What's the point in movin' us all about?" Tiny complained over dinner at Pat's. "Eeney and me have been hitting it off. You reckon this is the guv'nor's way of giving me a vote of no confidence?"

"It doesn't follow that you ride the horses you look after," Phil said, noisily finishing his pudding. "And it's not often the best training sense to keep one lad on the same horse for a long time."

"I know," Billy chirped with an evil grin. "Mr Harrup would quite like a winner, see? So ol' Tiny *has to* get the heave-ho."

Tiny didn't appreciate the joke. He glared balefully at Billy. Pat decided to douse argument. "I hate to say it, Tiny," he took up, "but the essence of what both Phil and Billy have said is true. Eeney's on the brink of a win and the guv'nor must assess all the permutations of lad-horse-rider. He's been longer in this game than any of us. He'll be taking into account the horse's form, the jockey's weight and fitness, the whole picture. And, whatever you might say about John, he is quite experienced at riding big races. You're fresh and eager, Tiny. You're a trier. But Eeney might need no more than a careful, solid ride – if you get my meaning."

"You think that John's the right man under those circumstances? Under *any*?" Billy wasn't joking this time.

Pat hedged, drumming his spoon on the table-top, pulling faces. Una watched him, smiling. "Oh, I dunno. John hasn't had many . . . er, falls. He's had a lot of tuition – "

"You've said it all, Pat." Billy's voice was blatantly cynical.

Pat rose, a little annoyed. "Look, you three. I don't know exactly what's got into you these last couple of days regarding John. OK, so he's not the most endearing of personalities. But he is the guv'nor's son and we all have to work with him." He fixed on Billy. "It'd be easier on yourself if you came to terms with that and got to . . . to like the fellow. Or at least tolerate quietly." Blank-faced indifference met his gaze. Billy just sighed. "What *is* up?" Pat asked. "What's the gripe? Is it something to do with Pete – ?"

Una interrupted, "Where is Pete? Seems we're seeing less and less of him."

"He's been extraordinarily busy," Billy said wryly, but Tiny shot her a warning look.

"I've heard about the unrest goin' on," Pat pursued. "Mr Harrup told me about the row the other day. Is that the tip of some iceberg? I'd like to know, lads. Remember, as far as the job's concerned, I'm the guv'nor's right-hand man. So if you have a grievance or something – "

"It's nothing at all," Billy said forcefully. "You're getting carried away, Pat. Everyone's just geared up for Monday, that's all. And Pete's been his usual self, keeping his horses company and working hard."

Pat gave a hurried run-down of tomorrow's duties, scribbling out a note for Pete and paying special attention to the four scheduled runners for Monday. He gave Pete's orders to Tiny, bade the group goodnight and turned for a whisky before bed.

Phil made straight for the hostel, but Billy paused with Tiny in the shelter of the bungalow doorway. They could see the dim light burning in the big stable and guessed Pete was there, as usual talking to Aura Lights. Tiny flicked Pat's notes. "Maybe I'll leave these on his pillow. No sense disturbing him."

"Yeah," Billy said ruefully, "he's had a tough enough day, what with helping John out and everything." She pounded a foot on the ground. "There's got to be a way to twist that meanness back on John. If only I could think – "

As they spoke Pete emerged from the stable and, to their surprise, came rushing towards them. "Did you see him?" he said urgently.

"Who?"

"John. Just now, a minute or two ago."

Tiny and Billy shook their heads in confusion. "Quick," Pete said, "there's something you must see. Come with me."

They ran to the big stable and down the centre aisle. Absolute stillness surrounded them, but one sound – a slow persistent crunching – was faintly audible. At Eeney's stall Pete stopped and pushed in. He held the door for the others. Tiny and Billy approached cautiously, ready for anything. At first everything seemed quite in order. Eeney was up and calm, his tail swishing happily. Then Billy blinked to take in the scene again.

"What's he eating?" she said. "That's feed in the manger – "

"Check it. Tell me if I'm wrong."

Billy and Tiny crouched and nudged Eeney away from the manger. Both dug their hands into the thick, stodgy feed. Tiny gasped. Billy said, "What's the game? This is mash. And it's not mash day, is it?"

"Even if it was," Tiny muttered, "you don't give mash to a

horse a few days before a race. That's a cardinal sin, the worst. I mean, you might as well run him lame again."

Billy swallowed hard. "Did John give him this, Pete?"

"Last night I was with Aura Lights at the other end of the stable and I thought I heard something down here, but I was tired out and half-asleep. I didn't check it. Tonight I heard the same rumblings going on. I sneaked a look out and there was John, all uptight-like, tip-toeing down with a pail. He emptied it into the manger then crept away like some sort of criminal. I thought it was unusual. Unusual for a start for John to be working this late. Even more unusual for him to bother feeding anything at this hour."

"It's weird," Tiny said smartly. "But important. We must let Pat know right away. All I can say is, I'm glad I'm not riding you now, boy."

"Why?" Billy asked.

"Because that puts the cap on it, Billy. If Eeney's been fed regularly on this stuff his race chances are all over. He can't win."

"I'll stay here, keep an eye out," Pete offered.

Tiny and Billy went back to the bungalow and disturbed Pat's bedtime drink. Una, in her dressing-gown and ready for bed, looked on as Tiny told about the discovery. Pat collapsed in a chair, utterly speechless. When he had regained himself he said, "This is incredible, too much to take in." He turned to Una. "What was I saying to you just the other day about Eeney's exercise schedule? I just couldn't believe there was any sense to it. The guv'nor seemed to be trying to disorient the horse – that's how it looked to me anyway. I asked him about it, but I thought it must be some new-fangled scheme he was trying. Then there was that incident with the bookie Hastings. Remember, Una. I told you I'd seen them acting suspiciously in Lambourn – "

"And John's assigned the ride," Billy put in. "C'mon, Pat, be frank. What sort of sense does that really make?"

Una suddenly broke in: "What Mr Harrup does is his own

business, Pat. I told you that before. He pays the wages, you remember."

"What is it, Pat?" Billy implored. "What d'you think is going on? Is the horse being got at seriously?"

"Well – " Pat was avoiding Una's harsh eye. "It does seem to me he may not after all want the horse to win."

"But that's insane," Tiny said. "What does he gain if Eeney loses?"

Pat had been long enough in the game to understand most of the tricks. "Quite a lot actually, if certain little wheels are put into motion – "

"But Eeney's fit to win," Billy insisted. "Just a little luck, and it's as good as done. Give 'im a good jockey – "

"OK, OK." Pat swallowed his whisky and stood. "You're pressing me for answers I don't have. Truth is, I don't know what the game is. Far as I'm concerned we're preparing Eeney to win. But feeding him mash makes nonsense of our work. It appears only John and Mr Harrup know the score, the real score. If I ask the guv'nor – "

"Which you're not going to do," Una warned. She came and stood between Pat and the lads. "This sounds awful, but it has to be said. If the guv'nor's up to trickery then we must leave him to it. It won't come back on any of us. Pat and I have discussed this, so it might as well be said. We must consider what's behind this possible fiddle. If Mr Harrup is trying to get some quick cash because he's skint and you come along and throw the spanner in the works – then think of the consequences. You might all find yourselves out of jobs. And it won't be so bad for you lot, but where will Pat and I find a good job with a house to go with it at a time like this? You tell me where."

Tiny shrank back but Billy said, "You think it's really this serious, Pat? That Rectory is against the wall?"

Pat nodded uncomfortably. "Apart from anything, lads, there isn't a lot we can do to change the guv'nor's plans. Even if we confront him he can tell us to mind our own business.

And that'll be the end of it." He poured himself another large drink while Una frowned disapproval. "Una's right. We've all got a lot to lose. Tiny's career. Billy's apprenticeship. Our *home*. It sickens me to think of it but we've got to face up. If Worcester is a cheat, then we must play along as part of it."

There seemed nothing more to say. Billy wasn't happy, but she had no choice other than to retreat with Tiny. Una stood staring mournfully after them, more than slightly embarrassed by her own outspokenness.

In the yard Billy hesitated, holding Tiny back. After a minute her expression brightened and she seemed pleased with some private thought. "What're you thinking about?" he asked nervously. "I don't like your grin."

"If this is Eeney's feed time, then we must see he eats. I'm going to give him some oats. Do it properly."

"We can't, Billy. You heard Pat. We've got to leave well alone. If John and the boss want Eeney to have mash, that's it."

"No. Pat may be right. Maybe we'll all lose our jobs. But I doubt it." Tiny went to plead again but she spun on him. "Look, Tiny, whatever is going on it's not right them treating a horse like this – "

"It won't do much harm. Just make him lazy and heavy."

"Well, it's not on. Eeney's a fine, beautiful animal. He's worked to earn his chance to win and I'm not standing by to see him messed about. Now John can go on playing his tricks with the mash – but it's going to end up as oats every night. I'll see to that. Pete loves animals. He'll come in with me, no question. It's up to you. You can turn your back and walk away here and now and I won't blame you. Or you can be a man and help out. Help Eeney."

Tiny took a few anxious minutes to make up his mind. "Hell, girl," he said, "you drive a hard bargain. Come on! Where do they keep the oats in this cow barn!"

*

It was the day before the race, and John was making a late return from exercising Eeney at the gallops. Harrup was striding towards the house as John pulled into the yard. "Everything OK?" Harrup mumbled, gesturing that he wanted no reply. Behind him, almost within earshot, Pat Devlin was tinkering with the motor of his mini-van.

But John leant down. "I'm not so sure. Eeney's perked up again. It almost seems as if – "

"Hush, boy," Harrup spat, glancing over his shoulder. In a low voice he added: "Can't you see Pat at the shed?" He came closer, troubled by John's frown. "What's the matter?"

"I dunno. He's just quickened up. Half the time today I was tearing him back."

"Rubbish. With all that mash he's been fed this last few days! He's bound to start dragging his hooves once you push him. On Thursday he looked terrible at the gallops. I was there, saw it myself."

"Yes, but you haven't seen him since. I tell you. It's all I can do to run him wide and make him jump awkwardly – "

"It's nerves," Harrup waved a dismissive hand. "Same as before every major race. People begin doubting everything." He saw that John was still distinctly uneasy and rested a comforting hand on his arm. "Mark me, laddie, I know my horses. Eeney looks like he's sickening. Tomorrow will be a walkover." He tried to distract his son. "Now, what about yourself? How're you feeling? Did I hear you complain yesterday of a sore shoulder?"

"It's fine. Just bumped it." John was coming down to earth. He relaxed in the saddle and smiled thinly. "Don't concern yourself about me," he said aloud, knowing Pat could hear. "I couldn't be more ready for the challenge. I'll give you exactly the performance you'll be looking for."

"That's my boy." Harrup slapped Eeney's rump. "I've just spoken to the other lads in the big stable. They're all set up for the morning. Pat'll be going along to Newbury with Gobbledegook and Just Nicola. That will be Pete and Phil

121

riding. Pete and Gobbledegook should make a great team. Pete has a way with that animal . . ." John made a mocking sigh. "Phil and Just Nicola will do well to make the first three, taking the field into account," Harrup continued unabashed. "As for Worcester – Tiny'll take out Misty in the 1.30. You'll be off, as you know, at 2.00. The girl Billy will look after your mount till the race." He stopped, looked carefully to make sure Pat was busying himself, then spoke quietly: "The girl has to ride out her other charges to exercise in the morning. She'll be safely out of the way between eight and eight-thirty. Don't forget to sneak a good bucket of water in to Eeney, and maybe some more mash. I'll give him more water just before the race, soon as I get the girl's back turned."

"Sure. And afterwards – ?"

"I remember." Harrup's face fell: he disliked being brow-beaten by anyone, no one more so than his own son. "After the race Billy gets her marching orders. I'm a man of my word, you know that."

Harrup turned for the house and John dismounted and led the gelding across to the stable. As soon as he entered the enclosed area the sense of hostility was overpowering. Phil, Pete, Tiny and Billy were working. They paused to glower, then went on with their various tasks. John spoke a loud defiant greeting and laughed boldly at the limp response. Billy was just finishing changing a gelding's straw and he collared her. "Here," he snapped, passing over Eeney's reins. "I'm told you'll be leading up for me tomorrow. You might as well get an early start. I'm in a bit of a hurry. You wouldn't mind stripping him down for me, would you? Good. You'll all be happy to know we've got a fine, fit beast here. I should be very surprised if he doesn't take the Dundeek Trophy tomorrow."

Everyone pretended not to hear. Billy chewed her lip, but held her tongue. She had been "looking after" Eeney – with the lads' help – for several days now. Another small chore or two would make little difference. She soothed the horse and took him into his stall, winking coolly to Tiny who was just raking in fresh bedding.

Pete was labouring away three stalls down, grooming Gobbledegook. Tiny and Billy could clearly hear John stop to interrupt him. "By the way, Pete, I got a very late start today and Tiger Tom needs a leg-stretch. Please look after that for me. And, in case the girl isn't competent, check over my tack tonight. I'm out for a drink so I won't have time to do it." There was a grim grin in the tone. "There's a good fellow." Tiny and Billy listened, but Pete didn't reply.

When John had gone, Billy strolled down to Gobble-degook's stall. Pete was kneeling, lovingly massaging the horse's legs. He looked depressed. Billy gently clapped his shoulder. "He's a pig, isn't he?" she said. "He deserves more than a tough ride from Eeney tomorrow."

Pete shrugged. "There's only so far you can push some-one," he said. "And I'm afraid I'm over the limit. I've had it." Billy tried to imagine pint-sized Pete physically tackling the sturdy John. She failed. But already Pete was expanding his plans: "I'm not prepared to eat out of his hand forever. So I guess I'll start looking for another job. It's the best way out."

"You could face Dobbin. Spill it all out to him."

"I doubt if that'd change much. John would still be around to nettle me, wouldn't he? No, I've had enough of him and of Rectory."

Disgruntled, Billy left the stall and ambled to the exit door. Tiny padded up beside her and leant heavily on the jamb. He saw she was deep in thought and said nothing for a minute. At last he said, "John's day will come."

"Yeah, but when? 1990?" She shook her head tensely, like a dog drying itself after a swim. "No, he'll have to learn. And I've got an idea."

"Oh no. What now?"

Billy's expression was fierce. "You can't race with a

hangover, can you? Nobody can. You said so yourself, Tiny. Last week up at the gallops. You said somethin' about it being like getting belted with a mallet – "

"What're you talking about?"

She twisted cheerfully to him. "I'm talking about a way to hit back at Dobbin *and* teach John a real lesson. What we've been doing with the feed guarantees that Eeney will be fit tomorrow. At worst John'll have a hard ride, but if they're out to lose he will pull Eeney up anyway. Right?" Tiny had no opportunity to say anything before Billy continued: "I'm going to make sure John *doesn't* ride tomorrow. Someone else will, and Eeney will have a real chance to win." Tiny went to launch an attack, but Billy raised a threatening fist. "Now don't give me this guff about losing our jobs if things go against Harrup. Like I said, I don't believe it. And anyway, things are bad enough already. Look at poor Pete. He's talking about quitting. It's not fair. I'm not looking for glory, Tiny, you know that. But someone's got to teach Rectory a lesson in decency."

"You're gonna' stop John riding then. How?" Tiny couldn't help but half-smile at the idea – he was in full sympathy with Billy. If only he had the guts . . .

"Tonight's our night in Lambourn. Let's get cracking and get our work finished quick. We'll hitch into town and I'll fill in the story on the way. Just do me one important favour."

"What's that?" Tiny's heart was sinking in anticipation. He had a premonition of what this was all about.

"Break into your piggy-bank and get all the money you can together. We're going to need it."

# TEN

Before leaving Rectory John had promised his father that he would go easy on the drink for the evening. "One shandy and a few orange juices," he had sworn. And he meant it. The most important thing a jockey needed just before a big race was a clear head. It was essential to ride to a plan. At the end of the day, even if he was bitterly defeated – as he knew he would be – people must say, *What a race! John Harrup really tried! The lad has talent*. Losing convincingly, John decided as he drove his motor-bike towards Lambourn, was probably more taxing than winning. He would need his wits about him tonight and tomorrow.

Avoiding his regular place – the rather posh *Tanner's Tavern* – he made for *The King's Cup*. Here it would be easier to skip the pitfall of familiar friends with bottomless wallets and a determination to get merry. A few of the regulars at *The King's Cup* were known to him. They were less well off, but easy company and light on the booze. Ideal companions for tonight. He parked his bike and went in.

Eric McCarron from Shentons' was quick to latch on to John, recognising an "easy touch". With a bit of luck, Eric reckoned, he wouldn't have to put his hand in his pocket for the rest of the evening. But somehow, however John worked it, Eric ended up buying the first drinks of the evening. The Space Invaders machine in the corner took their attention and Eric challenged John to a game. They played once – and John lost. And again, despite John's warnings of revenge, the second try gave victory to Eric. John finally kicked the machine. He stalked over to a corner table, still nursing his first shandy. Eric sat beside him, glass empty. Eric waited, but there was no positive response from John. In the end stark thirst got the better of him.

"Don't know about you," Eric said testily, "but I could do with another drink. The tension of those Invaders makes you sweat – " He stood to go to the bar.

"Lovely," John said. "Thanks a lot, I'll have an orange squash this time."

Eric cursed softly to himself and elbowed into the crowd. When he was gone John sat draining his drink. Suddenly, unexpectedly, a tall glass of beer was banged down in front of him. He glanced up at the two surprise faces beaming down. "Thought you might like something," Billy said. "Saw you polishing that lot off." She swung a leg, cowboy-fashion, over the back of a chair and plonked herself down. A grinning Tiny sat on John's other side. Both looked windswept and breathless. " 'Scuse us," Billy went on. "We've been doing a rather fast pub crawl. Lookin' for a, er, friend." Both she and Tiny raised their own drinks. "Well, cheers."

John sat motionless, frowning from one to the other. Unaccustomed as he was to their open-handed friendliness he was dumbstruck. At last he shuddered into life. He gazed at the beer. "I've just had a shandy, thanks. I, er – "

"Oh, come on," Billy appeared crestfallen. "We're all celebrating the big day tomorrow. Don't put a damper on it."

Eric arrived, equipped with two cheap watery-looking orange drinks. His eyes lit up when he saw the tall beers. "Eric, old pal," Tiny enthused, "let me get you a drink too. Beer all right?"

"Sure. Thanks, Tiny." He nodded nervously in acknowledgement of Billy's greeting. As Tiny marched off John prodded his beer forward. "Eric can have mine. I'm not – "

Billy pushed the glass firmly back. "That's not cricket, now, is it? Here's me and Tiny being nice and generous with you, burying the hatchet, saying, *let's all toast tomorrow's success.*"

"Go on," Eric nudged, "what're you waiting for . . . since someone else is buying the drinks?" He smiled to Billy. "I'll go along with that toast. Let bygones by bygones, eh?"

Tiny came back with the last beer and everyone started to drink, John with evident unease. As soon as the glass met Billy's lips it stayed there. In one draught the drink went down. John was suddenly embarrassed by his unmanly sip-sip-sipping. He took one long deep drink and emptied half his glass. Billy sat back, slightly dizzy. "Whew," she laughed, "that was good. It's always easier to stay sober when you do the first one or two pretty fast. Have you ever noticed that?"

Eric gave a world-weary shrug and Tiny hurried on to finish his. The next bit too was planned. There was some idle chat then, as John cleared his glass, Billy rose. "Let's have a chaser. What'll it be? Whiskies?"

Tiny took the bait freely. "Yes, I'll have another vodka and orange. I think. Might as well splash out good and proper since we have a few quid, eh? OK, boys?"

Eric was delighted but John was already mildly woozy. "I've had little or nothing to eat today, so I'd better be careful," he said. Then his eye caught Billy's and he saw her contempt. What was she thinking? That he was a yellow-belly, some sort of kid with no gut for alcohol? His fists flexed under the table. She had called his bluff before, during the whip incident in the tack room. Then he had looked an incapable, immature idiot. This time he wouldn't shirk her challenge. For a few minutes he worried about tomorrow's race, then he buried his concern. After all, he wasn't alone in riding tomorrow. Tiny was due out at Worcester too. So if Tiny could stomach it . . . He crushed his doubts aside. "All right, make it a whisky for me."

Billy sauntered to the bar and caught the eye of Jean, the girl assistant she had come to know well these last weeks. She craned towards her. "Right, Jean, I'm in business. Give me two whiskies neat. And two orange juices in vodka and orange glasses again." Jean grinned and passed them across. "You're about to see a miracle over at that side table," Billy said. "Ever see someone my size down a vodka and orange in five seconds – and stay sitting upright?"

"You'll rot in hell for this," Jean quipped.

"What? For being good and staying teetotal? Never."

Back at the table Billy swallowed her drink and Tiny made a convincing racing effort to beat her to it. But her glass was drained first. Eric then tried to match them. He took a mighty mouthful, put down the glass and gripped the table's edge. His eyes rolled in his head and his cheeks blew out like a goldfish. John, not to be outdone, gulped the whisky with little or no expression. Billy licked her lips and Tiny struck up a further rambling, pointless conversation. Only this time the participation from Eric and John was somewhat diminished. Both slumped, red-faced.

"I'll do the honours this time," Tiny said after a while. "More whiskies and vodkas, I think."

Eric found no tongue in his head to speak but John slurred, "Not for me, thanks. I'm quite happy – "

"Rubbish," Billy boomed, "we'll have the same again, Tiny. The night's still young." Eric fell forward, barely propping himself on jellied elbows. Billy examined John's face seriously. "You *are* all right?" she asked, all motherly concern. "I mean, you're used to alcohol?"

John rubbed sweat off his upper lip. Tiny was swaying in front of him. Or was he swaying? Was it an optical illusion caused by the dim alcove lights? He looked back at the girl. No, his focus was perfect. He was quite all right. Quite sober. In fact, he felt good – excellent. His thoughts were crystal clear and, yes, the night was still young. It was ridiculous to start treating oneself like fine bone china. Look at Tiny – eyes fresh, chirpy as ever. Look at Billy! Bright as a lark!

"Save yourself another journey," John joked to Tiny. "Make it doubles this time."

"Doubles it is."

Billy was talking and John was avidly listening but – extraordinarily – the words made no sense to him. He wondered as he downed the next whisky whether it was possible he was running the risk of getting a bit tipsy. The thought flitted through his mind, but was lost in an avalanche of drunken confusion.

*

"Can't I trust you to do one thing right for me?! What kind of idiot are you to go out and get yourself blind drunk the night before the vital race!"

The shouted words echoed and exploded inside John's head as he attempted, for the third time, to sit upright in his bed. He moved one leg, then the other – but again the appalling nausea swept over him and his head slammed. "Please," he murmured, "go away, will you? I'm ill."

Harrup ripped the curtains open so that brilliant wintry sunshine flooded his son's room. He took John by the shoulders and tried to yank him up. But John curled into a ball, clutching his stomach and groaning out loud. "I don't believe anyone could be so stupid!" Harrup ranted. "We talked it over five times. You know what's at stake – and yet you walk right out and get drunk." Again he grabbed John, and this time succeeded in dragging him from under the bedclothes. "I'm not having it, you hear. Get out and on your feet now. You're going to ride today whether you like it or not."

John stood shakily in his father's grip. His face was yellowish green and his eyes closed. Harrup held him for a second, but as soon as he let go John slumped down. He fell back on the bed. "I can't do it," he moaned. "My head, my stomach – I just can't."

"*Why*, John? Why?" Harrup knew he was talking to

himself. He tried reviving the boy by slapping his face. "I don't care how much you've to suffer. You're climbing into that saddle if I've to hoist you up myself." He made a final effort, and at last John stood of his own accord. There was a moment of dead stillness. Harrup examined his son's strained face. John paused, covered his mouth, then dashed for the bathroom to be sick.

Fifteen minutes later he was still there. Harrup sat on the bed and reviewed his prospects. He had forty minutes, no more, to arrange the departure for Worcester. In the next fifteen minutes the transporter would be calling to collect Eeney. Certainly it was too late, in every sense, to back out of the race. Favell, for a start, would never forgive him. Neither would Jerry Hastings who was, no doubt, looking forward to his "take". But the writing was on the wall: John was not well enough to ride. From his long experience of jockeys and race crises Harrup understood the impossibility of attempting to run a rider with a hangover. He'd be off at the second fence. That might not be so bad, but Rectory could do without the scandal of running an ailing jockey.

John shouted out some kind of apologetic grunt from the bathroom and Harrup found himself yelling, "If this blasted affair turns into a mess because of your idiocy I swear I'll make sure you never race again. You've had your chance, boy. It's the last you're going to get!"

He stormed out of the bedroom and went downstairs. He paced around tensely for a while, then decided. There was really no option. Tearing open the front door he saw Pat Devlin busily running from the bungalow. He called him over: "Pat, I need you for a minute. Come here, but get the girl first. I want her too."

*

In the big stable Tiny was showing a new discovery to Billy. "I'm sure it was Dobbin that done it," he was saying. "Dobbin was the only one round earlier." He hefted the

130

bucket of water again. "Right under Eeney's nose it was, and Eeney just about to dive in. Look, there's two gallons there. That's a fine way to start a runner on race day."

Billy was furious. "Good for you that you got it in time, Tiny. That's another point up to us and another down for the boss." She gave Eeney a fond slap and the gelding responded with a contented sigh. "Don't worry, boy. You're gonna' have a crack at victory today if it's the last thing any of us do."

The door creaked behind them and Pat beckoned. "Mr Harrup wants you, Billy. A matter of some urgency, it seems. We're both to go to the house immediately."

Billy stepped back, shocked. "W-why . . . why would he want me?" She glanced to Tiny who suddenly didn't want to know. Tiny nodded to Pat, mumbled "Excuse me" and vanished. Pat took Billy's arm and guided her towards the outer door. "I don't reckon we should keep the guv'nor waiting, not in the mood he's in just now." He checked his watch. "And time is running short if Eeney's to be ready for the transporter."

As they walked through the stable and out into the yard Billy thought to herself, *this is it; John's spilled the story about last night and I'm for the sack. I'll be packing my bags inside ten minutes. I'll never get to see Eeney run . . .*

Out of the blue Pat said, "For a horse that's been fed thick mash day after day Eeney looks remarkably spry, wouldn't you say?"

Billy wiped her nose in her sleeve. "Not my job to say."

"Good girl," Pat said quietly. "Keep up that standard of acting and you just might talk your way out of this." He winked as he pushed open Harrup's front door. "Whatever it is," he added.

They found Harrup alone in the study. On the desk was a cup of steaming coffee into which he was pouring rum. His face was starchy white. Without pleasantries he launched off, ignoring Billy, "Pat, we've got problems. My stupid kid got himself pie-eyed drunk last night. How and why I don't know nor care. But he's poorly. Couldn't even get himself out of bed without being sick. It's that bad. So the plans must be changed. Get Una to go along with Pete and Phil to Newbury. They're both well experienced, they'll be able to look after themselves. You're going to Worcester. Here's the girl's licence."

Pat didn't speak for a fraction. "Er, her licence? You mean you want *her* to ride the Dundeek Trophy?" He shook his head to clear it. "But, why don't you swap, say, Phil and her – ?"

"No. Don't go complicating things for me. I've got my reasons." He looked away from Pat. "I'm decided. She rides Eeney."

The room was moving around in huge, wonderful circles for Billy. She flopped against the wall as Harrup turned to address her. "Right, Billy, you heard all that. Now I know you're not very experienced, but I don't want you to be nervous. Eeney may not be . . . er, on best form. So I'll fully understand whatever happens. Pat will lead up for you and he'll advise you on what to do and who to see once you arrive at the course." He was drumming his fingers agitatedly, keeping one eye on the wall clock. "The only problem of course is Vic Favell. I don't want you to run into him, so be careful to steer well clear. I'll entertain him as best I can, keep him away from the paddock." He stood up quickly and finished his coffee. "OK, that's it. We'd all best get moving – "

"Hold on a moment, please." The words spoke themselves. Billy gave a little start as she realised both men were staring at her, anxiously. She could almost hear the electric clock ticking above the fireplace, hear the rumbling approach of the transporter. That wasn't anxiety etched on Harrup's face. It was desperation. There was a film of sweat on his brow.

"What is it, girl?"

"What about my apprenticeship?"

Harrup nearly shouted, but he caught a grip of himself. "Some other time, my dear – "

"If I'm good enough to ride in an important race for you I should be good enough for an apprenticeship, shouldn't I?"

Harrup stomped towards the door. "It's too late to talk about it now. See me tomorrow. Then I can fix up – "

*Fix up.* Billy jumped on the words. She had it: she had him cornered, and in front of the essential witness. He had committed himself. She tried to appear casual, but her heart was pounding. "It'll only take you five minutes to sign the papers. Why can't you do it now? If you think I'm good enough – "

"Oh, all right, girl." Harrup cursed softly and pulled at a drawer. "Let's get it over with. At least it will stop you nagging me endlessly." He flung down a pad of printed forms and began scribbling out details. Twice he stopped to take a hearty drink from the rum bottle. "Sit down you two," he said angrily. "I'll run through this with you, and Pat, you can witness it."

Billy sat. She watched Harrup fill in *Apprentice's Name: Hilary Ure*, and she felt like leaping around the room. A few minutes ago she had been steeling herself for the sack. But now, with the stroke of a pen, her goal was achieved. The weeks of wishing and working were over. She had made it.

Before she could grow smug with the thought Pat leant over. "Congratulations," he said. "Now all you've got to do is bring home a winner." He smiled wryly to her and in that instant she knew he understood. He understood all her secret trickery of the last week, all about the feed, all about John.

"I never dreamt it would be this way," Billy said truthfully.

Harrup slid over the form for her to sign and reached for the rum bottle.

# ELEVEN

Tiny didn't do too well, but he brought in Misty fifth in the 1.30. Billy only had time to run over and offer a few words of consolation, then Pat was frantically calling her back to the paddock. "Don't mind me," Tiny said. "You're mounted on the great hope. It's all clicked for you. You must feel marvellous."

"I don't. I've never felt so terrified in all my life. I didn't think it could be like this."

"What?"

"When it's just wishful thinking you're always in the winner's enclosure, grinning and drinking champagne. You forget about this part." She nodded across to a high board listing the runners and their prices. "No one told me I'd be competing against that kind of field. Some of those horses' names are legends to me."

Tiny pulled a funny face and tilted his helmet back. "Let me tell you a secret. You know how careful I am with my bets, eh? Remember the last time I took on Jeremy, then covered myself with Falcon Tony?" Billy nodded. "Well, today I've got a tenner on you, that's all. You're OK, kid. We're all with you."

Billy rode out to the starting area and Pat trotted alongside to give some final advice. Then she was alone, and all around her, slowly but surely, the other eleven horses were beginning to nose towards the starting line. The favourite, Pot of Gold and another short-odds runner were ranked next to her. The betting on Eeney, she knew, was shaky. The odds were short to begin with, but one or two bookies had lengthened them. According to Pat, a man called Hastings had started the scare. Pat had not seemed too surprised by this. In fact, when he told Billy he smiled wearily. Pot of Gold, Esquire and Candida M would be her main challengers. All were frequent winners over this two-and-a-half mile distance and all were on form. Pot of Gold had a master jockey up – the well-known Tommy O'Beirne.

Someone shouted an order and the horses moved to the starting-line. Tommy O'Beirne was beside her and he glanced over quickly. She caught her own reflection in his goggles. Her heart rose. She looked splendid, decked out in silky blue and gold with a white scarf at her throat. The sudden vision cheered her and she concentrated once again. Eeney was nervous and straining to go. She spoke to him, cool reassuring words pouring forth in a surprisingly calm voice. Then everything happened fast. All of a sudden they were under starter's orders, then they were off. A wild cry soared from the crowd.

Up in the members' box Favell gripped Harrup's arm. Harrup was exhausted. For a full hour he had laboured at keeping Favell busy and distracted. Fortunately Misty, another horse owned by him, was running too. That had helped. So had Favell's fondness for hard drinking. But now the owner's focus was fully back on Eeney. He checked his card in a hurry. "Did I hear someone say we had a change of jockey here?"

"Um, yes. I've got a new, er, girl . . ." Harrup rushed on: "Fine rider, just about the best I'll ever get."

Vic Favell seemed pleased enough. He stretched forward to watch the approach to the first fence. "Well, she's running him well. I have confidence in you, Jack. If I hadn't there wouldn't be one hundred and fifty pounds sitting on a win today." He turned to Harrup, seeking response.

"Seems fair enough," Harrup said grandly. "Can't see any

reason why Eeney should let us down. Can you?'' As he spoke he was standing on the tips of his toes, searching through binoculars. When he found Eeney he was instantly dismayed. Just as Favell said, the girl was riding superbly well, holding an ideal spot in a cluttered field. But that was not all. The gelding seemed happy to gallop free. There was none of the left-footedness he anticipated, no signs of tough effort. Harrup cursed himself, recalling the warning John had given yesterday. What exactly had the boy said? That the gelding's pace was *quickening*? But that was impossible, of course, with the diet he'd been on. No animal could sustain pace over so arduous a course with a stomach full of mash. Any minute now Eeney would start to falter.

"Nice one!" Vic Favell shouted as Billy took Eeney over the fence.

On the track Billy hardly felt as though she was riding at all. Eeney's gait was measured and precise and, without her directions, he seemed to know exactly what he was about. The second and third fences slipped past and the fourth saw a group of fallers on the inside rail. Immediately the field thinned out. Esquire, who had been running abreast with Eeney since the start, dropped back and Candida M took his place. Some other jet black gelding broke clear of them. But Pot of Gold held on to his position, right at the front. Behind Esquire there was a considerable gap – then the packed group of dawdlers.

The fifth jump passed without incident and suddenly they were approaching the half-way mark. Billy shook herself alert. She was allowing too much free rein, and Eeney was lagging. She looked round. Esquire was fading away but Candida M and the black gelding were making good ground on Pot of Gold. Already Eeney had lost two lengths to Candida M.

They approached the sixth at a general quickening beat. Pot of Gold stumbled and the crowd on the stands roared, aghast. Candida M took the lead, with the black gelding at its tail. Eeney overtook Pot of Gold and, for the first time, Billy settled to work. The slightest smack with the whip powered Eeney forward. Under her thighs Billy felt the coiled tension of the horse, and knew he had plenty in store. She tapped him briskly again and he went at the seventh like a rocket. Candida M went over first – then there was the horrible bunched charge as the black gelding, Eeney and Pot of Gold struggled to jump best and take the second spot. Despite her efforts Billy couldn't make it. Tommy O'Beirne cleverly brought Pot of Gold angularly across the fence, shutting off Eeney's chance to open up immediately on landing. Billy screamed silently in annoyance but cheered up when she saw the black gelding had fallen away. Now it was just the three of them – Candida M, Pot of Gold and Eeney.

Tiny had joined Pat on the stands. The thundering chant around them was for Pot of Gold, but the odd frenzied voice called Eeney's name. Tiny stood, tired but tense, closing his mind to the din. Speaking out his innermost thoughts he said, "Has she really got a chance to win?"

Pat slid his chewed cigarette from one side of his mouth to the other. He looked completely serene, statuelike. Tiny went on: "She told me on the way down that you knew the trick we played with the mash and all that. She felt bad in case you thought she'd done it all in order to get the ride herself. It wasn't like that. She . . . *we* only had Eeney's interests in mind. Billy, to give her due, was upset that the horse was being messed around – "

"I know," Pat cut in. "She's the best kind of horsewoman. She has her faults, but she *cares*."

"If this turns out sour," Tiny was watching his fingernails, not the race in progress, "will you hold it against us? I mean, you said it could mean you and Una out of house and home."

"I'm in this business for training winners, Tiny." Pat crushed out his cigarette and, without warning, let out a roaring cheer for Eeney. "There'd be no greater pleasure than to see that gelding cross the post first," he resumed quietly. "Let the future look after itself."

Comforted, Tiny turned back to the race.

The running was hectic now. With three fences to go, Candida M, Eeney and the favourite were still thrashing it out, with little sign of anyone weakening. It crossed Billy's mind very swiftly that old Dobbin must be heavy-sweating and counting his losses. It seemed certain that Eeney would at least make a first-three placing. The third fence from home was crossed easily. Faraway spectators saw what looked like three dead level mechanical horses speeding towards the close of a long track, each one in perfect step. Coming in to the second last fence Eeney ran a bit wide and it took a feat of mature strength to pull him back on course. But Billy lost a few strides. Pot of Gold and Candida M both observed the mistake and decided in unison now was the time to make the winning gallop. Billy cursed herself but refrained from the whip. Eeney himself knew what he had to do. She just spurred him gently and gripped tight as the massive muscles under her stretched and strained. Billy held her breath and counted down to the last fence. Candida M was directly in front of her now and Billy was obliged to pull left to clear the jump without obstruction. Pot of Gold was comfortably on the inside rail, sailing along. Billy saw Candida M start the last leap, then her concentration was back on Eeney. She urged Eeney up. "*Go, boy!*" It wasn't until she was in mid-air, flying over the fence, that Billy saw impending disaster. Inches away from her, but falling rapidly into her path, Candida M had lost balance. The young jockey knew what was happening and thought it better to jump free. Billy's brain registered the various actions: Eeney landing straight and speedy; Candida M rolling down, rump in the air; the young jockey diving clear. Billy had to decide a course – and she did so in a thousandth of a second. Crossing her reins, she prodded Eeney towards the short space between the falling horse and its rider. She ground her teeth and half-closed her eyes. Would she make it? Or would Candida M's hind legs trip her? She waited . . . and nothing happened. Shaking off the shock she reassessed her position. *Yes*, she was still there with a chance. Pot of Gold was running steady but, against the odds, she was no more than a length behind.

They were on the final straight now with three furlongs to go. Tommy O'Beirne had the edge of experience and he was pulling out all the stops, pumping a rhythm that seemed to lift his horse forward. But Billy tried harder than she'd ever done before. She abandoned the whip and started to talk Eeney home, whispering, pleading, daring. Eeney answered her by unleashing a storm of energy. With two furlongs to go they were side by side. Tommy was shouting wildly, begging more from the favourite. Billy heard nothing, only the silent, powerful body talk of her own mount. She felt herself gaining ever so slowly.

It was on the last furlong that the break was finally, brilliantly made. Pot of Gold had nothing else in store, but Eeney displayed his champion's reserve. Billy almost lost her grip with the sudden violent tug as the gelding burst forward. At the post he had gained a good length on Pot of Gold, as positive a win as anyone could hope for. Only then, as they zoomed past the finishing line did Billy allow herself the thrill of hearing the crowd's roar. The tangle of sounds was fabulous and intoxicating and for many minutes she wasn't quite sure it was all real. Someone ran up and patted the horse, grabbed her, planted a kiss on her cheek; somebody else called her a genius. Then Pat was running up, with Tiny at his heels. Pat held the bridle and punched her knee with a huge grin. "Do me a favour, Billy. Tell 'em you learnt all that from me."

She beamed down at him and dismounted with Tiny's help. She faced him and he bent away from her, unwilling to show too much delight. "That was all right," he grunted. "Bit messy over the last fence, but I reckon it'll do." He glanced earnestly to Pat. "Shouldn't be a photo call on that I guess, Pat?"

"Not unless they fell asleep in the box, Tiny," Pat laughed.

Tiny blushed and turned his head away. "That's it, then. First win of the season. But where's the guv'nor to enjoy it, eh?"

As Tiny was speaking, Harrup and Favell were making their way towards the finishing area, lost in the streaming crowds. Favell was bouncing along like a two-year-old, but Harrup, apparently, had suddenly come over ill. "Jack, you've done me proud at last. As good as your word. You'd promised he'd walk it, and walk it he did. With that starting price, I'm very happy with my takings for the day. I only hope you had a good wad on Eeney's nose too."

When they pushed through the crowd and found the winning team Favell momentarily recoiled in horror. "That girl – *her!* She's the one who – "

Billy hung her head but Pat stepped in. "The one who rode your winner, Mr Favell, yes. I think she did rather splendidly, don't you?"

Favell stuttered, "Um, well, the truth's before our eyes." His face split into a dazzling toothy grin. He shook Billy's hand. "I suppose what happened before . . . well, it's water under the bridge, isn't it? You've made up to me. You brought Eeney home. I'm . . . I'm grateful."

A press photographer bumped Favell's elbow. "If ya' wouldn't mind, guv. How's about lining up round the horse? The girl in the middle, right?"

Everyone shuffled around to pose and Pat walked self-consciously up to Harrup's side. They were silent for a minute as two or three flashbulbs popped, then Pat said, "How does it feel, guv'nor? We've been a long time waiting for this."

"It's great," Harrup said dully. "Great." The photo session was over and he ambled away. There was pride in his breast but bitterness clouded everything. The result was, of course, a disaster. He had made a desperate misjudgement and could not now avoid suffering the consequences. *If only,*

140

he repeated over and over, *if only I had trusted Rectory, trusted myself, trusted honesty* . . .

*

After the presentation of the Dundeek Trophy and the ensuing celebrations Jerry Hastings was waiting for Harrup in the car park. The famous frozen grin was conspicuously missing from his face and the gangster poise was all the more in evidence. He was leaning on the bonnet of Harrup's Landrover, smoking. Harrup saw him from afar and considered running, but he really had no choice. He advanced nervously.

Hastings stubbed out his cigarette on the tyre of the Landrover. His movements suggested menace. "I shouldn't have listened to you, Jack," he said evenly, "should I? After the last one was such a close-run thing, I should have been wary. I don't know how well you know your horses and your riders, mate, but take a tip from me: they're better than you give 'em credit for."

Harrup spread his hands in apology. "What can I say? There was a last-minute hitch with the jockey . . . the horse just took off . . . the girl rider was too good . . ." He flopped jadedly against the car. "I'm sorry, Jerry. Just in case you think this was some kind of weird joke or double-cross – forget it. I hadn't a ha'penny on that horse."

"You owe me three thousand, son. That was the hand-out total for me, I'm afraid."

"I . . . I haven't got it, you know that."

Hastings clicked his tongue impatiently. "OK, you said as much last week." He kicked the Landrover with a heel. "Well, I've got a car. I don't want a new one but – like we agreed – you can sell this. That should cover the three amply."

Harrup had been terrified of this moment. He was shaking, and not from the frosty cold, when he said, "It's not mine, Jerry. I-I should have come clean with you. I've only

141

made a couple of payments on it, so it's not mine to sell."

There was murder in Hastings's eyes. He gazed hard at Harrup, teeth clenched. "Then it was a con job, chum, wasn't it? You tried to manipulate *me* to help feather your nest, eh? Look, sonny, this may come as a surprise to you but I *earn* my living. All right, now and then I dabble in a bit of side-dealing. But I work to make ends meet. I *work*. If you're not fit or capable enough, then it's not my task to hold you up. I'm sorry, Jack, but I don't like double-dealing. You offered me something and I accepted. I want no sob stories, I want what's rightly mine." He dusted down his overcoat and adjusted the hat on his head. "I don't care what you have to sell. I want my three thousand. I'll give you two weeks to raise it." There was a sudden change in his level tone. He stood inches away from Harrup, so close that the tobacco on his breath could be smelled. "For the good of your health, Jack – make sure you come up with the cash. Get it?"

Harrup pulled open the door of the Landrover as thunder rolled and the skies opened. Rain lashed the ground. In a half-hour the earth would be pitted and soft. If Eeney had been running later everything might have been different. But the die was cast now. The past – and his hopes – were dead and done with.

*

None of the lads saw it coming. For days after the big win all talk had centred on Worcester and Newbury, and riding lessons learnt and mistakes made. Pat and the others seemed to purposely veer away from discussion about repercussions and the stables' future. Instead they analysed performances. Phil had failed miserably with Just Nicola and Pete had only managed a fourth position with Gobbledegook. Tiny's fifth placing was a disappointment too. But weighed against these, Billy's victory balanced the books. Everyone rejoiced in reliving the race conversationally. It was unanimously agreed that no more suitable rider could have been mounted on Eeney that day. Billy was champion class.

*

Six mornings after Worcester, the axe fell. Una came to the hostel with the rumour at six-thirty and when Tiny and Billy led out the first exercise string at seven-fifteen the reality was there before their eyes. A large hoarding erected near the gate announced: *For Sale By Auction – Rectory Training Stables – Viewing By Appointment*.

"That's it then," Tiny sighed from the heart. "Una was right, we're all to have our marching orders. Rectory's finished."

Billy was feeling sorry for herself. "The story of my life," she grumbled. "I break my back working, and just as things begin to turn out for me they go wrong. I've struggled for this apprenticeship, won a great race . . . and now it's snatched away."

"You've only yourself to blame. Same for us all, I guess. Pat dropped enough hints. We knew in our bones how things were going – "

"But we did right. We were learning horse training, not corruption."

Tiny laughed spontaneously, though he was feeling cold and glum. "I have to hand it to you. You're unrelenting to the end, aren't you? Everything's just simply black or white, right or wrong. There's no in-betweens. You know exactly where you're going and what you want." He spurred his mount to keep pace with her as they left the Sparsholt road and headed for the gallops. "So tell me, Miss Know-all," he said with a chuckle. "What determined ambitions will come to fruition next?"

Billy took the question seriously. She settled in the saddle and smoothed Eeney's mane. "First I beg, borrow or steal a job I can hold on to. And then – well, look out Willie Carson! I'm aiming for the stars."